MENDING
WORDS
with the billionaire

OTHER BOOKS BY LORIN GRACE

American Homespun Series

Waking Lucy

Remembering Anna

Reforming Elizabeth

Healing Sarah

Artists & Billionaires

Mending Fences

Mending Christmas

Mending Walls

Mending Images

Mending Hearts

Artists & Billionaires 5

MENDING WORDS
with the billionaire

LORIN GRACE

CURRANT
CREEK PRESS

Cover Design © 2018 LJP Creative
Photos © Deposit Photos, Fred Russo on Unsplash

Formatting by LJP Creative
Edits by Eschler Editing and Valerie Bybee

Published by Currant Creek Press
North Logan, Utah

First edition: November 2018
ISBN: 978-1-970148-00-8

For Nanette
THANK YOU FOR FIXING MY WORDS.

ZOE TURNED THE PRINTED MOCK-UP of the magazine layout upside down, squinted to make the image blur, then fully opened her eyes. As she suspected, the nose in the illustration sat too high and the title font needed to be a few points smaller. At the computer, she made the necessary adjustments. A+ worthy work. Hopefully her professor agreed.

A tap sounded on Zoe's door. "Dr. Christensen is on the phone for you." Candace handed Zoe her cell.

"This is Zoe."

"Sorry to call you on Candace's phone. I couldn't access your number since you are not currently one of my students."

"One of the issues with keeping my number unlisted." Zoe gave an apologetic shrug to Candace. To be precise, when she'd transferred up here, she'd asked the university to keep her information as private as possible.

"I'll get to the point. Adrian Scott, one of my friends in New York, of Scott & Ricks—"

Zoe restrained from gasping and tried to concentrate. Scott & Ricks was one of New York's premiere advertising and design companies.

Still, she missed some of what Dr. Christensen said. "—he asked if I had any students who could fill the position on short notice, and I thought of you. After checking with the other faculty, they agree. Although you are a transfer student, you would represent our graphic design program the best. I know you have Tessa's wedding next week. It was so nice of her to invite me, too. Adrian is willing to have you postpone until the day after Labor Day. That only gives you two weeks to make arrangements. Would you like the position?"

Zoe's mind raced, trying to figure out what she'd missed in her excitement.

"Zoe, are you there?"

"Sorry. Yes, I am trying to make sure I understand—a job with Scott & Ricks?"

"Internship. A favor to the school and me. The college wants to launch a graduate program in graphic design, and having this sort of internship helps give us credibility. I know you completed most of your studies elsewhere and wanted to graduate in December. I think completing your degree can still be arranged between the internship credits and a guided-studies online course. Your other professors and I can coordinate your work with Adrian Scott's team. There is a small stipend with the internship, basically enough to not starve and not end up living in a homeless shelter."

"I don't know what to say. An internship in New York—it's unbelievable."

Professor Christensen laughed. "There is only one right answer. This *is* Scott & Ricks."

"Then I'll take it. NYC, here I come!"

"I'll email you the specifics. Make an appointment with your academic adviser in the next day or so, and we can get your credits worked out for graduation. I'll send her an email so she knows what we are trying to do."

"Thank you for thinking of me, Dr. Christensen." Zoe hung up and handed the phone back to Candace.

"New York? Do I officially have no roommates this fall?" Candace took a seat on the bed.

"Sorry, cuz. I can't pass up an internship in New York with one of the foremost design companies in the country. Eeek! Two weeks!" Zoe bounced out of her chair.

Candace smiled. "You don't look sorry. Just don't go finding yourself some Wall Street mogul. Then the curse will be complete. It's like I have the Midas touch. Every roommate I have ever had in this house has married someone whose income exceeds the GDP of Tonga."

"No way am I joining that club. You know how I feel about following trends. And I am not going there to date." Zoe had no intention of getting into any relationship, ever. The last time she thought she was following her heart, life had taken a major detour, convincing her that love was a lie. Her sense of direction in relationships eclipsed her lack of sense of direction in general. No map or GPS could help. "If anyone is going to continue the trend, it would be you. Isn't Colin Ogilvie worth at least $5 billion more than Daniel? You would end up the richest of us all."

"We. Are. Just. Friends. So stop it." Candace left the room before Zoe could apologize. The ongoing argument was getting as old as it was pointless. Perhaps seven hundred miles between them would change how they ended their never-ending quarrel.

Zoe turned back to her computer, singing the famous Frank Sinatra song. *"If I can make it … New York! New York!"*

Nick Gooding sat across from Sean Cavanaugh, going over the contract. Sean looked out the window as often as a third grader on the last day of school. The view of the East River from the office window was not nearly as attention-grabbing as his friend found the scene to be. "Your mind is wandering again."

"Tell me yours wouldn't if you were getting married in twelve days to the most remarkable woman you've ever met."

Nick shook his head. His friend was done for. A more significant part of him that he would never admit was jealous. Sean had found the one thing money couldn't buy—love. Money could demand respect, inspire awe, and wield power, but in finding true friendship, money became a burden, and in seeking love, money could become a curse ten times more potent than one dug up with an Egyptian mummy. Sean had no idea how lucky he was. "I envy you. Tessa is perfect for you. I wondered if she could navigate your newfound wealth, but it seems to me she is the voice of reason—both in when to spend and when not to."

"Oh, that reminds me. I am keeping the old apartment until the end of the year. I need to let my accountant or assistant or someone know to pay the rent." Sean pulled out a phone and swiped the screen.

"Why? I thought you two just got the apartment mostly cleaned out." The two-bedroom rent-controlled apartment Sean's mother grew up in had been hard for him to let go. At one point, he had considered buying the building the apartment was in, but Nick had pointed out that the older building wasn't the best investment if Sean wanted to get into Manhattan real estate.

"One of Tessa's roommates, Zoe—you'll meet her at the wedding—got an unexpected internship starting after Labor Day. Finding housing on short notice and an even shorter budget in the city is nasty, so we offered her a trade. If she finishes painting the apartment, the place is hers until Christmas. It's a win-win and saves me hiring a painter to get rid of the olive-green kitchen I never updated."

"Your mother never updated the place either. You know you are a billionaire now. You can just pay to have the work done and let your assistant deal with the hiring." Nick flipped to the next contract left by the legal team. "You are still thinking of buying the building, aren't you?"

"You know I am. Since I am going to have to move out of Granda's house, I feel like I am losing my roots. And some major remodeling would give us a nice place in town when we need to be here. I don't know if I could ever do one of those penthouses with the black and white."

"Hey, are you dissing my pad?"

Sean laughed. "Central Park South penthouses aren't for every billionaire."

"It beats living with my parents. Not that I don't like Blue Pines, but right now I prefer the city."

"Tessa still can't get used to the idea of a housekeeper or staff of any sort. If we didn't have such a problem with gawkers and solicitors, we would be happy with Granda's old house now that the years of paper collection are cleaned out." A lovesick smile plastered Sean's face.

Nick would trade his penthouse, the apartment in Paris, and almost everything else he owned if he could feel like Sean did about a woman and know she felt the same about him. "Let's finish up with these contracts. I think you are going to be useless the rest of the week."

Sean didn't argue.

Nick slid a paper across the desk. If only he could be as useless. But he had other things on his plate to worry about. For months, the statistics had been on the front page of every magazine and newspaper in the country. #MeToo had prompted his father, Ansley, to have their lawyers take a hard look at the various company policies where they were invested as well as the systems within their own enterprises. They audited their entire portfolio of businesses, every passed-over case of harassment examined. At first Nick had doubted the need for reviews and training, but after months of interviewing, he wished there had never been one.

two

ZOE SIGHED AS SHE WATCHED the bride and groom kiss for the first time as husband and wife. The wedding had been everything she'd dreamed of as a little girl. Sean's grandfather officiated, his advice blending serious and loving with a dash of humor. Radiant in her wedding dress, Tessa represented an ancient goddess of love and beauty.

Candace handed Tessa back her bouquet, and Tessa and Sean began the recessional. Zoe waited for her cue, then took the arm of the groomsman, following the others down the aisle to the doors of the church. She barely glanced at the man at her side. He was handsome, polite, and rich. Why couldn't she have been partnered with one of the other men? Neither was wealthy. The pub owner was irreverent enough to be off-putting, and the other was too tall for her taste.

From the second she had been introduced to Nick Gooding, the zing of attraction had zapped her. Nodding and smiling at the well-wishers, Zoe did her best to ignore the electric current running up her arm. After all, too much electricity could kill, and she had been burned before.

The newlyweds and their attendants exited the chapel, then gathered on the steps for the various photographers and cameramen to memorialize the moment before climbing into the horse-drawn carriages for the ride to the museum for dinner and the reception.

Nick sat next to Zoe. "I get the distinct impression you'd like to be someplace else, perhaps with someone else."

Zoe cringed. She hoped she hadn't been that obvious. Between her roommates' teasing from the last two nights and her natural reluctance to be paired with any man, Zoe had done exactly what her mother had warned her not to do. Be rude. "It's not you. I mean, I don't even know you after only two days of wedding stuff." She bit her lip, searching for an answer that was graceful and kind. "It is the curse of the Art House. I am the only one of Candace's roommates to avoid dating a millionaire or billionaire, and when they realized I was paired with you for the wedding, they started teasing … and well, I am not going to succumb to the curse."

"Curse?" Nick raised his eyebrows and adjusted his cuff links.

"Candace says the curse is her own Midas touch. Every room-mate she has ever had is married to someone who is a gazillionaire of some kind. I mean, look at Sean. He didn't even have money when Tessa fell for him. It's a curse."

"All of them?"

"There were two roommates a couple years ago—one married this guy who designed an app, the other a tech mogul in Boston. Then there are Mandy and Daniel Crawford, Araceli and Kyle Evans, and Abbie and Preston Harmon, who are all here."

"Are your other roommate and Colin Ogilvie together too?" He glanced at the carriage behind them where the maid of honor rode with his old friend instead of the best man, who was with his wife and daughter.

"My cousin Candace and Colin? That relationship is compli-cated. Very complicated. I wouldn't say there are wedding bells anytime soon, but who knows?" Out of loyalty to her cousin, she would say no more.

Nick nodded. "I have two sisters. I can imagine how much you got teased this week since you are the only unattached female in the wedding party."

"Probably more than you could ever imagine."

"So, because I'm single and wealthy, you are going to spend the rest of the day avoiding me?"

When he said the words like that, avoiding him didn't seem like such a good plan, but she nodded.

"Well, I guess that is a relief. I was beginning to wonder if I had something hideous stuck in my teeth or some other repulsive feature."

Zoe turned her full attention to him. "Oh no. You are not repulsive at all!"

Nick laughed.

Zoe felt her cheeks heat. At least she hadn't admitted just how attractive she found him.

"And I haven't been rude or offended you in some way?"

She shook her head. "No, you have been perfectly polite. I am afraid I am the only one who has been rude. I didn't mean to offend you."

"I am not offended. Usually my money has the opposite effect on women. For the sake of the bride and groom, do you think you could pretend I got a text from my banker informing me bandana-clad outlaws broke in and took off with all my gold? I believe we still have photos and an obligatory dance before the night is over, and the photo will be better if we appear friendly."

"You keep gold in a bank?"

A rich, warm laugh nearly as potent as a hug came from deep inside him. Even his laugh was appealing. "Not anymore."

There was still the problem of the electricity between them, enough to power a Tesla, but not for all his money would she admit she was aware of it. "Well, if your money is gone, I have no reason to fear the curse. I apologize for being so childish. The fact that they all fell for men with money is a coincidence, after all. It wouldn't be possible for there to be a curse anyway."

Nick leaned into her shoulder. "What if it isn't a curse? It could be a blessing."

She was still avoiding him, though not as openly as before. He suspected she was hiding behind the supposed need to hold the Crawford's baby, Joy, so the couple could dance or sit with Reverend Cavanagh. It was something more than teasing over a curse, he realized, as she'd avoided dancing with the other groomsmen as well. Perhaps she also felt the magnetic pull between them. At the rehearsal dinner, he thought he'd imagined his reaction to her, or perhaps it was the triple chocolate dessert. On the carriage ride over, the sparks flew again, even as she ignored him. Nick finished his dance with Sean's mother and escorted her off the floor.

"Would you mind getting me a cup of the lemon water? I seem to be older than I thought." She took a seat next to Revered Cavanagh.

"Do either of you need anything?" asked Nick.

Both men shook their heads.

In the refreshment area, he found Colin Ogilvie on a similar errand.

"Ogilvie, I had no idea you could dance like that. Next time I get one of those invitations to be on *Dancing with Divas*, I'll refer them to you."

Colin frowned. "Please, no. I only can dance with Candace."

Something in Colin's voice gave Nick pause. "Is everything all right?"

"Just tired of the friend zone."

"Candace?" He'd observed Tessa's friend with the ever-changing hair interacting with his old school chum all week.

Colin accepted two water glasses from the wait staff. "Who else? I was hoping now that she will be roommate-less, I could get her to come to Chicago more, but she is more averse to change than anyone I have ever met."

"I thought Zoe lived with her. Wait—she is the one with the internship, right? Doesn't she have other roommates?"

"Candace hasn't been replacing her roommates."

The waiter handed Nick the lemon water he'd requested. Nick took a napkin as well.

"What is up with you and Zoe? Has she pulled one of her disappearing acts?"

Interesting. Perhaps Zoe was an introvert. "You were paying attention to us? Let me guess—friend-zone problems?"

"Candace was an introvert. She is very protective of Zoe."

"I am not sure we are even at friendly. She is keeping to herself." It was more like trying to get into Fort Knox.

"She is a Wilson woman. Runs in the family. Good luck." Colin raised one of the water glasses before walking in the direction of the tables.

If Colin noticed something between Zoe and him, Nick knew he hadn't imagined the attraction. When it came to people, Colin was about as unobservant as they came.

Nick gave the water to Sean's mother and went in search of Zoe. He found her in a dim hallway holding baby Joy to her shoulder.

Zoe spotted him and held a finger to her lips, then walked toward him using the same swaying motion his older sister used when rocking her children to sleep. "What?" she mouthed.

"I thought I'd see where you disappeared to."

Zoe smiled at him and slowly turned back down the hallway. He heard a set of heels approaching.

"There you are. Tessa is almost ready to toss the bouquet. Mandy sent me to find my granddaughter." A woman in her mid-sixties skirted around Nick to Zoe's side. They exchanged the sleeping child without waking her, the baby smiling in her sleep as she settled into the older woman's arms.

Nick offered his arm to escort Zoe back to the main reception.

Zoe glanced over her shoulder. "That's Bonnie, Daniel's former secretary, personal assistant, and mother hen. She insisted on coming since Mandy's mother had to go back to South America. I think Bonnie has pretty much adopted Joy."

"Tessa must have too, to make her the honorary flower girl." Nick opened the door into the grand gallery.

"It may have been an excuse to get Joy a matching dress, or three. This is the second one Joy has worn today."

Nick admired Zoe's dress. "Do the bridesmaids get multiple dresses too?"

Zoe shook her head. "Just the one. We have matching T-shirts from our hen party."

"That is the oddest name for a party." Nick led her to the dance floor without asking and spun her into the waltz position.

"Probably. I have no idea where the name came from. Mandy preferred the name to bachelorette, since she felt that was synonymous with bar hopping." Zoe followed each of his turns flawlessly. "And everyone since has followed suit."

"I noticed the distinct lack of alcohol at the wedding." The dry wedding saved the celebration from the inevitable guest who imbibed too much and embarrassed the bride or groom with a declaration of unrequited love.

"I am not sure Tessa ever drank. 'No alcohol' is one of Candace's rules for the Art House." Zoe spun away from him and back.

"Your cousin makes no-drinking rules for college students, and everyone abides by them?" Nick didn't consider himself much of a drinker, but trying to picture his college fraternity alcohol-free was a stretch.

"Get to know Candace a bit and you'll understand." She shrugged under his hold. "Our little college is ranked in the top-twenty of stone-cold sober universities since Candace started her crusade. It isn't even a religious school. My cousin is stronger than a force of nature." He could feel her relax as she spoke of her cousin.

"So, what does she do?" Nick asked, hoping to catch her in another moment of unguarded candor, but the music ended and Zoe stepped out of his arms.

"She is an artist like the rest of us."

The band leader spoke over the chatter. "Okay, all you single ladies. It's time for the new Mrs. Cavanagh to toss the bouquet. If you will gather at the bottom of the stairs."

Candace walked up and linked arms with Zoe. "Come on, cuz. If I have to, you have to."

"Fine, but I am not catching it. That is your job." Zoe put her arm around her cousin's waist and walked in the direction of the grand stairway.

Nick wandered over to where the single men were gathered. Michael O'Malley speculated who would catch it. "If that hazel-eyed farm girl catches it, stay out of my way for the garter toss. I'd like a date with her."

It took Nick a minute to realize he spoke of Zoe. O'Malley was harmless enough. However, he went through women as fast as he did Irish stew on a Friday night rush at his restaurant. Nick sized up his competition. If Zoe caught the bouquet, O'Malley wouldn't have a chance. The garter and date would be his.

three

"REMEMBER THE DEAL. I DUCK and you catch it." Candace tugged Zoe into position.

"How can you be so sure it will come your way?"

"My sister's wedding, Mandy's, Araceli's, and Abbie's." Candace counted off the names on her fingers. "I am not catching the bouquet a fifth time."

"I don't think Abbie's wedding should count since she threw the flowers at you as she ran from the room to follow Mandy to the hospital. It wasn't a real flower toss. I could argue she wanted you to hold them."

Candace pushed Zoe forward. "I am not doing this a fifth time."

"Have you ever considered that the universe might be telling you something?"

"Not happening. Not in my plan."

Zoe grabbed Candace's hand and looked her in the eye. "Maybe you have been wrong for the last ten years and it's time to change your plan."

"Maybe you have been wrong for the last two years and you should change yours."

Tessa climbed up to the third step. "Ready, ladies?" Before turning her back to the assembled hopefuls, she looked in Candace's direction.

As soon as Tessa turned her back, Candace stepped out of the way, leaving Zoe little choice other than to catch the flowers or be pelted in the face. She glared at her cousin. Tessa blinked back the surprise on her face when she turned around, then clapped for Zoe.

Zoe posed next to Tessa for a photo before the announcer called for the bachelors to gather around. First in line was Sean's grandfather. Tessa sat in a chair and raised her skirts a few inches. Sean snagged the garter and shot it like a rubber band over the group of men. Reverend Cavanagh lost his attempt to snatch the piece of lace out of the air to Nick Gooding.

Zoe felt the weight of all her roommates' eyes on her. Every teasing remark from the last week slammed into her brain.

"Breathe. He is a nice guy, and the billionaire thing is all super-stition." Tessa squeezed Zoe's shoulders in a half hug before nudging her in Nick's direction.

Nick held out his hand. "We get to start this dance."

The announcer called for all the single ladies and gents to join them. Soon the floor overflowed with dancers, and Nick spun Zoe to the edge. "Do you need to sit down? All the color drained from your face when you caught the flowers. I thought you might faint."

She attempted to smile. "I'm fine."

Nick raised a brow but didn't comment. He danced them along the perimeter of the floor. When the song ended, he escorted her to a seat at the corner table.

"We have a tradition around here. I owe you a date. What would you like to do? The sky is the limit." He sat next to her.

Why did all the rich guys have to be handsome? Zoe knew she was better off without handsome or rich. To be honest, she was better off without anyone for now. "Since they stole all your gold, I am not going to take that literally."

"What? No skydiving onto the Statue of Liberty?"

She crossed her legs and adjusted her skirts. A server came by, and she took a water. "Isn't that illegal?"

"Probably. So the sky is the limit within FAA-approved flying areas." Nick asked for a cola. Colin and Candace joined them.

"How about you take me for an ice cream cone?" It was the simplest date she could think of. Even in New York, a double scoop should be convenient and quick.

Colin shook his head. "Seriously? An ice cream cone? At least get a Broadway show out of the deal since you'll be living here for the next few months."

Nick turned to Zoe. "What about a show and an ice cream cone?"

She looked to Candace before answering. Her cousin's encouraging smile was no help.

"I think an ice cream cone will fulfill your obligation."

Candace made a face Zoe hoped the others didn't see.

"Well, then, ice cream it is." Nick agreed without hesitating.

Perhaps she should have been more specific. Nick had agreed too quickly.

Once the guests filtered out after the departure of the bride and groom, Nick and Colin moved outside to watch the bridesmaids leave in a limo.

"Are you staying at the inn?" Nick followed Colin back into the museum.

"Yes. I didn't want to stay in the city."

"Come out to the family house with me. There is plenty of room, and the remainder of the wedding party isn't on the floor above you." Nick didn't know Colin as well as he did Daniel. After seeing him interact with Candace over the week, he felt Colin could use some time away from the rest of the bridal party.

"That sounds like a deal I can't pass up."

Nick pulled out his keys. "My car is around back. Let's go get your things."

The estate covered a little more than ten acres—not vast by any means. Since over half of the land was covered in trees, the property afforded the Gooding family more than enough privacy.

Colin gave a low whistle as the house came into view. "My mother would kill for a place like this. She is forever complaining our home is too modern for her ."

"Welcome to the Cottage. Someday I'll be the fifth generation of Goodings to own it. Right now, the place is still my father's primary residence, although he and Mom spend almost as much time elsewhere as they do here."

"Are your parents here today?"

"I think so. They were at Sean's wedding. My sisters are both here someplace as they didn't want to miss the wedding either."

"Sisters?"

"Emma is married. I am not sure if she flew home or not. She didn't want to bring her children, nor did she want to leave them. Kaylee was the one in the red dress who danced with the guy with the goatee all evening. There isn't an official engagement yet."

"You sound like you don't approve." Colin grabbed his suitcase and followed Nick.

"I can't say I do, but I don't get any say in the matter." Nick indicated that Colin should leave his suitcase with the butler who'd greeted them. "He'll get that up to your room. Do you want the grand tour or just the shortest way to my man cave?"

A yawn proceeded Colin's answer. "I think the man cave sounds good for now."

"So, how long have you been dating Candace?"

"You mean how long have I been trying to date Candace? That woman has more tricks to keep a relationship in the friend zone than the Pentagon has to keep hackers out. The Pentagon is easier to hack."

"I am not sure I want to know about that."

"I was only twelve. Thanks to Dad's money, they didn't make

a big deal of the break-in other than making me create a fix for the hack I'd exposed. Why are women so difficult?"

"I have no idea. Zoe is interesting, but she can't stand me because of my money. Usually, women who know me have the money thing the other way around."

Colin took a soda from the mini bar. "Zoe has a talent for shutting down a guy even before he expresses interest. I am surprised she even danced with you at all."

"Really? Do you know why?" Nick settled into his favorite chair.

"Not a clue, and I'll warn you—don't even try to get any information out of any of the Art House women. They keep each other's secrets better than Area 51. Took me weeks to get Candace to tell me about her alopecia, and I already knew she worked with children with cancer. Other than she had chemo, I still have no clue as to the extent or the reason."

"You mean you have never tried to find out? With your hacking skills …"

"I could but haven't and won't. I am cautious about what side of the line I stay on. For some reason, Daniel thinks I cross the line more often than I do. Although to keep Mandy safe when they were first dating, I may have let things get a bit gray. Death threats tend to push those lines."

"How long have you been interested in Candace?"

"Since I first saw her spiky pink hair on my computer screen a year ago last March. 512 days."

It was Nick's turn to give a whistle of appreciation. "And she won't date you?"

"Nope. I tried for a kiss last New Year's Eve and came up all cheek. The annoying thing is I know about all these guys she has kissed. Not that she has kissed anyone since some law-student activist dumped her to go protest in California. She tries to keep me in the friend zone by talking about the guys she's dated like I am one of the Art House women. The guys she's kissed don't know her at all. She never lets them see anything beyond her rotating wig collection before she moves on."

"That explains a lot. I thought I saw her the other day down on the square. Since her hair was different, I thought I was mistaken."

"My favorite wig is a blonde with green ends. Ombre or something, they call it. It's soft and sassy, just like her."

"Oh, you have it bad. What are you going to do?"

"I need a new idea. Maybe you can help."

Nick spent the next hour brainstorming with Colin. His friend had reached the desperate stage. Coming up with ideas to help someone else was ten times easier than solving his own problems. "I think I have an idea. A couple years ago I purchased a two-story turn-of-the-century carousel. My thought was to fix the merry-go-round up and donate it to, well ... that doesn't matter. I still have the carousel packed away in a warehouse. The wooden animals need a lot of work. If I found the right artist ..."

"I have a new warehouse—nice and clean, state-of-the-art ventilation. It's never been used and is just the place to undertake the major refurbishment of an antique."

"Now if you only knew an artist. Maybe one with spiky pink hair. Then I would be happy to send the carousel out to Chicago."

Colin grinned. "Nick Do-Gooder Gooding, you are a genius."

"Now, do you have any ideas about how to break the ice with her cousin?"

WHEN ZOE FIRST THOUGHT OF finding a place in Manhattan, she figured she would end up with a shared studio that had leaking water pipes and would cost her the stipend she got for the internship. Sean's childhood home was far from that. The two bedrooms were small, and if she were a chef, the galley kitchen would be inadequate, but the 980-square-foot, third-floor apartment was more space than she ever dreamed she could have in the city.

All her friends, excluding Tessa and Sean, had helped her move her few boxes in. Since Sean had emptied the apartment of all but a few things, he'd given her an allowance to rent some furniture to add to the old couch and scarred kitchen table that remained.

Mandy walked through the rooms. "You shouldn't need much. A bed, a comfortable chair, a dresser. Daniel gave me the name of the company he used to furnish the apartment he had last year, along with a designer *not* to work with. Although her first attempt of orange, yellows, and purples might be your style. He said the rental furniture is good, just not the designer."

"I think the striped-animal decor was so much better." Candace laughed.

"What am I missing?" asked Zoe.

"Daniel lived here for about a month and decided to get an apartment rather than keep living in a hotel. The decorator he hired must have been a flunky from some reality show. Although at the time, I thought she was the Karma he deserved. He let the place go when the lease was up. We keep talking about getting an apartment here in New York, especially now that Sean and Tessa will be living here. I don't know if we will, though. Daniel's father hated the city, and Daniel can't see spending the money." Mandy measured one of the windows. "If Sean buys this building and turns it into a couple of condos, we'll be tempted to buy one. For some reason, Nick keeps talking Sean out of the purchase."

Zoe felt her spine stiffen at the mention of Nick's name. "Why should Nick have any say?"

Araceli sat on the couch. "Tessa says Nick wants Sean to take a year to get used to his wealth. This building isn't the best investment, for some reason. I think it's sweet that Nick is helping Sean through his new world."

"Because discovering you're a billionaire is hard?" Zoe couldn't keep the sarcasm out of her voice. Everyone turned to stare.

Abbie closed the refrigerator door. "Money is more of a burden than most people think. There is a lot of responsibility that comes with wealth because one can do so much harm or good. When I met Preston, I thought he was just a spoiled, rich guy. But he isn't. Yes, he grew up with a different lifestyle. Like Mandy, I want to raise my children close to me, not at some boarding school."

"Wait, what?" Candace narrowed her eyes and went to stand in front of Abbie. "Out with it. You have only been married for seven weeks."

"Eight, and yes, we are having a honeymoon baby. I'm already thirty-one, and I didn't see a reason to wait. Fortunately, Preston didn't either." Abbie placed her hand on her abdomen.

Mandy squealed and hugged her former bodyguard. "Have a girl. She will only be nine months younger than Joy. We can have so much fun!"

Both women turned to Araceli.

"Do you have any news?" asked Mandy.

Araceli held up her hands and shook her head. "Don't look at me like that. We are still living in a third-world country for another month, maybe two. We are waiting until we get back to consistent medical care and where Zika isn't a threat. Kyle's mom had difficulty with all her pregnancies from day one, and that isn't a risk we are willing to take. Besides, mosquito netting is a stumbling block to romance."

Zoe covered her ears. "TMI."

The women laughed.

Candace changed the subject. "So, how are you going to repaint? Painting was part of the deal, wasn't it? Does Sean want something normal or more like Art House?" Nothing could be like the Art House, with its murals and maze of hallways created by years of art students.

"I think I'll start with the kitchen. Anything will be better than this olive. Tessa picked out a yellow. I don't think she trusted Sean."

Two hours later, Zoe was left walking through a furniture store with only Candace. Araceli had caught a plane back to Haiti. Preston and Daniel had both texted their wives and taken Abbie and Mandy off to various places. After purchasing a new bed to be delivered that afternoon, Zoe only needed a couple more items.

Candace ran her hand over a bookcase in the second store. "I still can't believe everyone is moving on so fast. I didn't see Abbie ever getting married. I thought she would be a safe roommate."

"I'll be back." Zoe turned over a price tag.

"I bet you a semester's rent that Scott & Ricks hires you as soon as you get your diploma in December. You won't be back."

Zoe smiled. "Wouldn't that be wonderful? Scott & Ricks is the kind of place every freshman hopes to work when they graduate. But this is not Indiana. I am not naive enough to think living in the city will be easy. I am such a country mouse."

"The old song says, if you can make it here, you can make it anywhere." Candace sat in a chair. "Oh, try this one."

Zoe tried the upholstered recliner. "What are you going to do since you turned down the teaching job?"

"I have a few commissions lined up. Not as many as I would like, but I have enough work for now." Candace sat in a different chair, shaking her head as she got up.

"Have you considered selling Art House?" Another chair caught Zoe's eye. She might not get a job at Scott & Ricks, but with graduation in December, she would move on anyway, maybe to Fort Wayne or South Bend.

"Why? Where would I go? I have an amazing studio space and everything I need."

"Including two empty bedrooms? Three if you count mine." Zoe raised her brow. "I think I'll take this chair."

"Mandy comes down regularly." Candace took on the pensive tone that came more often as summer progressed.

"Do you think she will close up her little house now that they have a mansion under construction closer to Chicago? She already travels less because of Joy." Zoe wrote down the ID number of the chair.

Candace didn't answer.

"You had your ten-year plan and your bucket list. Check, check, and double check. It's time for a new plan. You know as well as the rest of us that Colin wants more than friendship."

"No. I can't. You and I may have different reasons for remaining single, but mine are just as valid."

"A decade has shown your reasons may be wrong." Zoe opened a drawer in a dresser, wondering if she could get by without one.

Candace took a step closer. "Just because I am here having this discussion with you doesn't mean my reasons have changed. And what about yours? Not every man in the world is a selfish jerk. Perhaps your reasons need to change too."

Zoe glared at her cousin. This was getting way too personal for the middle of a furniture store. "My reasons are never going to change."

"Mine can't." A tear formed near the corner of Candace's eye.

"You don't know that, things are already different." Zoe crossed her arms, desperate to get Candace to believe in a future she thought to be lost.

Candace rushed out of the store.

Zoe exited just as Candace was climbing into the back of a cab. Pedestrians streamed by.

She shrank back against the building and tried to figure out what to do next.

After seeing Colin off, Nick returned to his penthouse. Of all the men in his acquaintance, Colin would win the title "Least likely to be in the nine-zeros club." Although Nick suspected he was in the ten-zeros club. For Colin, if the subject wasn't related to a computer, it didn't exist. Well, other than Candace. She was good for him. Got him to leave his bat cave or whatever he lived in more often. Socialization had never been Nick's problem. If anything, he had too many friends. However, few of them were close, and more than a few only wanted to be associated with the Gooding name.

The place was spotless as always. His current part-time house-keeper was the best he'd ever had. He knew he would find the refrigerator full of enough food to have an impromptu gathering of friends this weekend if he chose. But this Saturday, he didn't feel like having anyone over. Maybe the need for privacy was the result of all the events of Sean's wedding and seeing the close friendships there, especially among Tessa's old roommates. Not once did they say anything catty behind each other's backs. Uncommon among many of the women he knew. Maybe growing up in the Midwest with middle-class families had taught them kindness. So that was this week's excuse. What was the reason last week and the week before?

He grabbed a water and headed out to his balcony, which overlooked the south end of Central Park. As soon as it had come on the market, he'd snagged the penthouse at the former Plaza Hotel. Not that he didn't like the Cottage, but he thrived in the city. Unconsciously, his gaze traveled to the west side of the park in the direction of Sean's old apartment. How was Zoe settling in? Nick scrolled through his contacts only to realize he'd never gotten Zoe's number. Tessa would have Zoe's contact information, but he wouldn't interrupt their honeymoon for that. Sean would never let him live the blunder down. He texted Colin knowing he probably wouldn't hear back until his friend's plane landed in Chicago.

Now, to plan an ice cream date that would last longer than grabbing a cone from Old Fellows, even if their strawberry ice cream ranked among the top in the country. He could show her around Manhattan. That would give them a few hours together.

By the time Colin answered his text, Nick had a foolproof date planned.

Hi, Zoe, it's Nick. Settled in yet? How about I show you around the city with our ice cream cone?

He hit Send and waited.

And waited.

And waited.

He hadn't anticipated needing a dose of Colin's patience so soon, but one thing he'd learned dealing in real estate was that waiting had its own rewards.

ZOE'S PHONE PINGED.

She wasn't ready to talk to her cousin yet, so she ignored it. The small grocery store had a surprising variety of foods, but the crowded aisles made her understand why many people ordered online. Next week she would try that. Carrying home a gallon of milk and two bags of groceries was not very fun either. At least she had opted not to get staples like flour and sugar this trip. The extra ten pounds would have done her in.

Zoe passed a corner florist. She should buy herself a bouquet like the girls in the movies. Determined not to look like the Indiana farm girl she was, her binge-watching of the last two weeks had consisted entirely of movies and shows set in New York, just not the crime shows. They would not be helpful at all.

The drab-olive refrigerator looked better with food inside it. Zoe couldn't help but wonder how the forty-year-old relic still worked. She opened the box to one of her favorite frozen meals and discovered another thing the apartment lacked—a microwave. In the cupboard above the fridge, she found a cookie sheet that may have predated all the appliances. She set the pan in the center of the small oven and turned the knob. She heard a rapid clicking sound, but nothing else seemed to happen. Zoe closed the oven door and waited. Maybe the flame needed to wait a moment. She found spots in the empty cabinets for the rest of her groceries.

Rotten eggs?

Zoe sniffed again. Gas! She hurried to turn the oven off. What should she do? Call 911? Zoe opened the kitchen window and grabbed her phone. Who would know? Growing up, she'd only had electric ovens. Even Grandma had owned one since the '50s. The ancient thing would often send out an electrical pulse guaranteed to shock anyone standing too close to the metal-edged countertops. Zoe opened the window in the living room as well before unlocking her phone screen. The internet should tell her what to do.

Nick's text popped up on the top of her notifications. Would he know? Probably not, but he might have a housekeeper or someone who would.

Do you know what to do when you turn on a gas stove and it doesn't light?

—Turn it off!!! How long was it on? Are you still in the apartment?

3 minutes maybe?

—Open the windows.

Did that.

—Call the super.

The super what?

—The superintendent.

Oh. I don't know where to find his number.

—He used to live in the apartment on the left when you go down into the basement.

Ok.

Zoe ran down the stairs and knocked on the door, which was helpfully labeled "Superintendent."

He isn't home.

—Why don't you come over here for dinner? I live in the old Plaza Hotel on the south side of the park. Any cabbie would know the address.

Zoe walked back up the stairs, not sure how to answer. She assumed he lived alone. If Candace was here, they could both go, but the fight would come back up.

No, thanks. I'll wander around until the gas dissipates.

—Around the corner to your left is Lucinda's. Order the soup of the day and the brioche bread pudding for dessert. You'll thank me later.

K. Thanks.

—Please get the super to check your pilot light before trying to cook again.

I will.

Zoe ran back upstairs to check the door to the apartment. As she hoped, she'd remembered to lock it. A rumble in her middle sent her in search of Nick's recommendation. After leaving the building, she walked down the stairs and turned right. The restaurant on the corner had an Italian name. Two more right turns later, Zoe found Lucinda's Café. She checked her texts, wanting to tell Nick he was wrong about the directions. Left. Zoe sighed. Well, at least she hadn't made a fool of herself by texting back.

"Zoe!"

She turned toward the voice. What was he doing here?

"Finished so soon?" Nick reached her side.

"No, I was just going in."

He checked his watch. "You didn't go back in the apartment, did you?"

"I took the scenic route to the café."

Nick held open the door. "Well, then, I am just in time."

"In time for what?"

"To see the look on your face when you try the food here."

They ordered at the counter. Nick set down a fifty before Zoe could dig any money out of her pocket. "My treat."

She followed him to the table and slid onto the bench opposite him. At least this would take care of their ice cream cone date.

29

"You have a smudge here." Nick pointed to a spot on his own cheekbone. "Looks like the old oven got you."

Zoe raised her hand to her cheek. She must be a mess.

"No, other side." He leaned across and rubbed his thumb across her cheek.

Electricity shot through her, freezing her in place until he removed his hand.

Nick made a face. "I think I made it worse."

Zoe's hand flew to her cheek.

"The restrooms are back there." He nodded, indicating the direction.

The bathroom mirror showed more problems than just the black smudge. Her hair stuck out at odd angles from her messy bun, and her mascara was smeared under her right eye. Probably from the cry she'd had after Candace left the furniture store. She restored what damage she could with water and paper towel. Good thing she wasn't trying to impress Nick. She rubbed at the black smear on her cheek again. What had been wrong with her when he'd tried to clean off the smudge? It was grease. Perhaps the electric feeling was some odd static thing amplified by the oily stain. By the time she returned to the table, her soup awaited her.

"Did you find the furniture you needed?"

"I found some. However, I didn't get any ordered."

"Why not?"

Zoe stirred her soup. "Candace and I exchanged some words, and I didn't finish getting furniture."

Nick nodded and ate. The impression he would have said more but was holding back filled the space between them.

Zoe tried to find a subject to fill it. "Have you heard of Scott & Ricks?"

"I have used them on several of our accounts. Their PR arm takes care of the Gooding public relations. They rent five floors in one of my buildings."

She locked her jaw to keep the water she drank from spewing out. "Your buildings?"

Nick smiled. "I may have lied when I said the bank called and someone stole all my money. I have several investments, including office buildings."

"Oh. So if I ever get locked out of the building, you have the keys?"

Nick made a show of patting his pockets. "Not on me. But I know who to call to get you in. Most of my buildings have electronic keys anyway, along with state-of-the-art security when needed."

"If you own real estate, why would you discourage Sean from buying his old building?"

"At the moment, the building isn't a good investment. The owner has raised the price, hoping Sean will buy out of sentimentality. After Sean walked away from negotiations, the price dropped by over a million. The other reason is I think Sean needs to understand what he is getting himself into before he jumps into real estate or any other venture. Sean wants the brownstone for sentimental reasons, and he could have a charming private residence if he used the top two floors of the building or even the entire thing."

"That would be huge."

"The building was built as a single-family home."

"That still seems like a lot of room."

"They did have large kitchens and staff as well as families with more than 1.8 children." Nick finished his soup. "The biggest obstacle he will have is there is one other rent-controlled apartment in the building. However, with the right enticements, the tenant can usually be persuaded to move elsewhere."

Zoe finished her soup and exchanged her bowl for her dessert plate. Nick sat back in his seat and watched her.

"You are making me nervous."

He raised a brow. "Why?"

"What if I don't like it?"

"Are you allergic to any foods?"

"No."

"Then you will like it."

"Confident much?"

He answered with a smile.

Zoe took her first bite. She wasn't going to thank him. By the time she returned to Indiana, she would gain ten pounds off this dessert alone.

"Told you that you would like it."

"Has anyone told you you're annoying when you are right?"

"Other than my sisters, no."

Zoe savored another bite. "Do me a favor, don't introduce me to any more amazing foods while I am here."

"We still have to get an ice cream cone, and Old Fellows is ranked among the top thirty in the nation."

Zoe shook her head and used her fork to point to her dessert. "No, you paid for this. You have completed your date obligation."

"This was not a date. This was a fortuitous meeting of friends."

"If that is all dinner was, you would have let me pay for my dinner."

Nick finished his brioche. "That wouldn't be very gentlemanly of me. You are, after all, a damsel in distress, chased from your apartment in an attempt to make your dinner. I rescued you from going to bed hungry."

Zoe rolled her eyes.

"You do that a lot."

"What?"

Nick slowly rolled his eyes and let out an exaggerated puff of air.

"I do not." Lie. Candace told her the same thing at least once a week.

Nick laughed.

Zoe finished her dessert.

"Let me walk you back. If the super isn't home, I have someone I can call to check the oven out."

Since the alternative was possibly waking up dead, Zoe agreed.

The super still didn't answer his door.

Nick pulled out his phone and texted his personal assistant.

Did you find someone to check out the oven?

—Yes. Just waiting for your call.

Please send them over.

—ETA 10–15 minutes.

Thanks

"Let's go walk around the block. Someone will be here in ten minutes or so to look at the oven. If it doesn't check out, can you go back to Blue Pines with your friends for the night?"

"I checked out of the inn. I guess I can go up there and see if I still smell gas."

"If the oven is leaking, with the windows open, you might not smell the danger. And don't roll your eyes at me. Tessa will kill me if I let you die while they are on their honeymoon."

"She wouldn't do that."

"Well, I am not risking it. She now has enough money to take out a hefty contract on my head."

Zoe laughed. "She isn't like that."

"Maybe. Maybe not. Has she had a friend die before due to negligence?"

Zoe shrugged. "I doubt it."

"Then I am not taking a chance." They walked around a dog walker. A little fluffy one strained at her leash, trying to greet them. A larger one watered a tree. A third dog eyed them as if trying to decide whether they were worthy of being barked at. It was the same look Zoe had used with Nick half the night. Whether or not she liked it, he was her only acquaintance in the city. Too bad she was so prickly. He had a feeling they could be friends if she'd pull in her quills.

"Do you often spend your Saturday nights rescuing random damsels in distress?"

"No. But you aren't random either. You are the woman I am taking on my next date."

Zoe didn't answer for a minute. In the shadows cast by the buildings, he couldn't tell what her reaction was. He was sure he'd received another eye roll. "So once we go get ice cream, you will no longer need to rush to my aid."

Nick turned and walked backward so he faced her. "I hope by then we will be acquainted enough you will call me a friend."

Zoe looked him in the eye and nodded.

Nick turned back around. A truck with the logo of a familiar contractor was double-parked in front of the brownstone. "Our help has arrived."

"You'll stay while they fix it?"

"Of course."

Zoe took a deep breath and relaxed her shoulders before taking out her key and letting them in the building. Nick wondered if it was the gas or something else bothering her.

ZOE SAT ON THE EDGE of her bed, staring at her phone. She pulled up Candace's number and sent the text.

I'm sorry.

The reply was immediate.

—Me too.

The tune "Lean on Me" played. Zoe answered her phone.

Candace started without preamble. "I was going to call when you texted. I'm sorry I went there."

"Me too. You may be partially right. I realized tonight that I am too scared to find out. It is easier to ignore things, you know?" Zoe lay back and studied the ceiling. It needed painting too.

"How did you come to that conclusion?"

"Nick Gooding said something about becoming friends, and I didn't know how to answer. I used to have straight guy friends, but now—"

"I understand. From everything Tessa and Sean have said about Nick, he is a good guy. If you choose to risk letting a guy into your life, he wouldn't be a bad one."

"What if—" Zoe let the sentence die.

"It is scary, isn't it? Colin left early for some reason. I'm wondering if you are not right about me. It has been ten years and two

35

months since I made my ten-year plan. Maybe I should make one for another ten years."

"Could you include Colin in it?"

"Maybe, but only as a friend."

Zoe wanted to slap some sense into her cousin, but she kept her voice neutral. "How much does he know?"

"Enough. More than most men who have not been part of my medical team. I told him about my mom. He knows I volunteer with pediatric cancer patients, but he doesn't know specifics."

Urging Candace to tell Colin about her past would probably lead to another round of silence. Zoe changed the subject. "So, Nick bought me all new appliances tonight."

"What? Why?"

"I didn't check the pilot light when I tried to use the oven. Didn't know I needed to. A seal had disintegrated, and the unit was so old the part wasn't available. Somehow that led to the old refrigerator not matching and the fact that there was no microwave, which is why I used the oven. I didn't think anyone could purchase new appliances after seven on a Saturday. He says he'll send the bill to Sean."

"So you had a man in your apartment alone?"

"We were never alone. There was a contractor and his helpers. Then the super came up, and I met three of my neighbors. There is this nice grandma type, Mrs. Clark, who lives below me. I think she was upset about the noise until we told her the oven was leaking gas. Then she offered us cookies. The super was a bit unhappy we were changing the appliances, until Nick handed him a business card, and the super left."

Candace sighed. "After all the roommates and Colin, you'd think I would get used to how much a name or money can accomplish, but I never do. I sure do appreciate it, though."

"When do you fly out?" Zoe went to check the lock on the apartment door again.

"Tomorrow morning. We would have left today, but Preston owed Abbie the show they missed in Boston, so they saw the one playing on Broadway. I was going to go with Colin. I don't understand why he left."

Zoe didn't comment. "I hope you have a good flight."

"Preston's plane. How could we not?"

The luxury jet had a bedroom and a bathroom with a walk-in shower. The seats were heaven. Having a lousy flight in his plane would be hard. "I think I am getting spoiled with all the private jets this year. I don't know what to do when I come back in December and have to fly commercial."

Candace laughed. "I know the feeling. Good night, cuz. Love you."

"Love you too."

The clunk of ice dropping in the ice maker startled Zoe. In the galley kitchen, she admired the new appliances again. Nick would have purchased some high-tech refrigerator that sent a grocery list to the delivery service, but she had pointed out it would be a waste of Sean's money since she would only be here for four months. The one he purchased was still beyond what he should have.

Her phone pinged.

Nick's text flashed across the screen. **How is 2:00 for our ice cream outing?**

Okay, where should we meet?

—I'll pick you up. This is a date, remember?

How could she forget the date? It was the first one she'd had in over two years. **See you at two.**

—Good night.

Thanks for the help, and good night to you too.

It wasn't until Zoe climbed into the new bed that the realization that this was the first night of her life she would be in a house or apartment alone hit her full force.

Feeling uneasy, she opened her phone to the ebook app and read until her eyelids closed.

Sometime after midnight, a cat screamed.

At 1:27, several sirens wailed.

Around four-thirty, her old nightmare returned after a fourteen-month hiatus.

Zoe opened the app again and read until her alarm went off.

The mirror told the story of her sleepless night. She hoped Nick wouldn't notice the extra layer of makeup.

Nick parked the car.

"This doesn't look like a place that sells ice cream." Zoe reached for her door handle.

He stopped her with a touch on the arm. "Let me get your door. Date, remember? And don't roll your eyes while I am walking around the car."

She rolled her eyes before he got out.

Nick smiled as he opened the car door. "This is the tour of the city I promised."

"It is a helicopter."

"The fastest way to see all five boroughs."

Zoe's steps slowed. "This isn't what I agreed to."

"Ice cream and a tour of the city?"

"It's over the top. Literally."

Nick stopped and studied her. "You don't like me spending money on you, do you?"

She squinted up at him. "Not really. Well, not at all."

"Well, I booked the tour for an hour. It doesn't matter if you get in or not, the helicopter is paid for an hour tour. Does that change your mind?"

"I'll go this time, but, Nick, if we are going to be friends, the relationship needs to be equal, split bill and all that."

"Fair enough. Nothing extravagant."

"Thanks." Zoe preceded him to the helicopter.

Nick couldn't help smiling. At least he hadn't taken her to Vermont to see how one of New England's more famous ice creams was made like he'd originally planned. Being Zoe's friend was going to be harder than he thought.

They buckled in, and the pilot gave them instructions. Nick spent most of the tour watching Zoe's reactions from the corner of his eye because whenever she caught him looking at her, she would point out the window to redirect his attention. The pilot hovered over the south end of Central Park for a moment while Nick pointed out the building he lived in and the location of Sean's apartment. When they flew farther south, he also showed her the building where Scott & Ricks was located.

"Have you figured out how to get there tomorrow?"

"Last week Tessa helped me get a metro card and we all took a field trip to the office from the apartment. My sense of direction isn't the best, so they wanted to be sure I wouldn't get lost. As long as I remember to change lines at the right place, I should be fine."

"If you ever get lost, give me a call."

"Thanks."

The flight concluded with a view of the Statue of Liberty. Zoe took a photo with her phone. "Thank you for the tour. The city is amazing from above. I am sure I will never forget it."

After they got their ice cream cones, Nick took her on a walking tour around the south end of Central Park.

He stopped in front of the Plaza Hotel. "Do you want to come up and see where Eloise lived?"

Zoe bit her lip and shook her head.

"Then at least come in the building. The Plaza is one of the city's treasures."

She stopped in the lobby and did a slow turn. "Wow, I officially feel like the country mouse."

"I felt the same way I when I moved in. But when I saw the condo penthouse for sale, there was no way I could pass the place up. What kid doesn't dream of living in a hotel after reading the books?"

"I watched the movie over and over again. I was sad for her because even though it was a fun adventure, she didn't have a real family, at least not much of one." Zoe followed him, peeking inside the restaurants and shops.

"Do you have a large family?"

"I am the second of five children, so some people call seven large. Dad is a farmer, so that should cement my place as a country mouse."

"Brothers? Sisters?"

"All brothers. I have one older brother and three younger. That is probably why I am so close to Candace, even though she is four years older than I am. I always wanted to be like her. I suffered through years of ballet lessons or, rather, my teachers did, because she was a ballerina. Then, when she quit and turned to art, I did too. Eventually, she stopped treating me like a little pain of a shadow, and we became friends. She convinced me to find my own niche. Thankfully, I discovered graphic design. It's a much better fit for me." They browsed through the shops.

Zoe picked up a doll, checked the tag, set it back down, then did the same to a smaller version.

Nick picked up the larger one and took the doll to the register.

Zoe left the shop while he made his purchase. Nick located her outside the window of the next store. He handed her the bag.

She peeked inside and handed the bag back. "You just don't get it, do you?" She turned in the direction of the lobby and hurried away.

Sighing, Nick thought about returning the doll but didn't want to deal with it. Besides, he could put the doll in the room with the Eloise painting.

He needed advice. How was he supposed to impress a woman who didn't want things?

seven

"AND HERE IS YOUR CUBICLE. The computer is a thousand years old, so if it gives you any problems, hit it. The bottom drawer locks. The key should be in the top drawer. Though we haven't had many problems with theft in the office, the pranking can get pretty bad if there is a deadline. And cell phones are not allowed on the floor." James shook his head. His bleached, blue-tipped hair didn't move. "My cubicle is next to yours. Until IT gets up here to give you your passwords, you can pull in a chair and I will catch you up on a couple of the projects we are working on. For now, you will be doing stock-photo research for them anyway. If you want to impress Gina and get to some real design work, the faster you can find the thing she imagines, the better."

"How do you do that?"

"It helps to be part psychic." James led her into his own space. Various prints were pinned to the cloth walls. Zoe guessed he was about a year or two older. He spoke with a slight accent. "I tried to find out as much as I could about the projects before I researched, especially if they had done any concepts. Some clients have color preferences and style guides. When you get your computer, you will find you have access to most of them. Make sure you read the guides."

Zoe nodded. The lights overhead flashed twice, and a chime on James's computer dinged. Other computers on the floor echoed the same sound. "What is that?"

"Call to the Monday morning meeting, which is being held on Tuesday due to Labor Day. Oh, and the lights flash because April is deaf. She reads lips. Since she isn't always at her computer, the lights are set to notify her. She has a couple of signals we all find useful."

Zoe followed James back to a central area lined with couches and chairs. People shook her hand and introduced themselves. Names flew too fast to memorize. The woman who introduced herself as Gina welcomed Zoe to the team and started the meeting.

Zoe attempted to take notes.

James leaned over and whispered, "Don't bother. Everything with a deadline will be in the follow-up memo. Just listen and learn."

Projects were discussed and assigned. Teams were formed for two new projects. Zoe was put on one for a new food line with Gina and James.

Gina consulted a tablet. "Zoe, I want you to spend an hour or so shadowing each of us. Seeing what we are working on will help you get to know us and our projects, our working habits, etc. Everyone should have signed up for a time slot, which you will find on your calendar. Has IT been up here yet?"

"Not yet," answered Zoe.

"Well, you will be with me after the meeting. If we still haven't seen them, I'll send another message. You need a tablet as well as your passwords." Gina made eye contact with every team member. "Anything else?"

There were a few head shakes.

"Then, remember, this is a four-day work week, so it will feel like six. And Wayne will not be back until next Monday, so Adrian or Shayne may come down and visit us to see how we are doing without our beloved art director."

A shift in the atmosphere caused Zoe to study the faces around her. Something in Gina's last sentence had thrown everyone off kilter. Obviously, Scott & Ricks was not immune to office politics.

Zoe shook a few more hands as the meeting ended before following Gina to her office. "I wish you had your tablet. I sent another message to IT. Anyway, let's begin."

By lunchtime, Zoe's head was swimming. And it was a beautiful thing.

Tuesdays after holidays always put Nick in an odd mood. He rechecked the calendar before signing the last of the papers his lawyer had sent over. There were a couple of events at the 9/11 memorial, including the Tribute in Light, he needed to go to. Sean and Tessa would be back on the morning of the tenth. On the eleventh, he needed to be in Blue Pines for the dedication of the 9/11 room at the museum featuring the artwork of Sean's father, Cameron, who had given his life as a firefighter rescuing people from the towers. The museum board directed visitors to the other art from first responders or their families that would be part of the permanent exhibit. Tessa had created a stained-glass window that was being installed today so Sean wouldn't see it until the dedication. Nick needed to get to Blue Pines so he could check on it. He'd even had to reassure her during their short dance at her wedding reception that the window would be taken care of while they were on their honeymoon. Brides should not have to worry about such things. He made notes for himself and his assistant.

He added a memo to make sure Reverend Cavanagh and Sean's mom, as well as his family, arranged things so they would be in attendance. Zoe. He had forgotten to ask her to come. Would she even be able to get the time off since she was an intern? He could call Adrian and pull some strings, although Zoe might refuse to go if she knew he had. He had never met someone so determined to be stubborn. She was Tessa's former roommate … maybe the museum board could invite her.

Nick climbed into the back of the town car, glad his driver, Sebastian, had the responsibility for getting them through the afternoon traffic to his next meeting. Not for the first time he wondered what a different life would be like. Zoe's reaction to the doll still bothered him. His sister had been no help. To her, a date without a gift wasn't a date. Was his life so different from the rest of the world? He ate and slept too. He loved. Well, not recently, outside of his family. He laughed. Not since Sunday afternoon, but he did. There had to be thousands of women in the city who were of marriageable age. Judging by the letters his PA had round filed, more than a few were willing to go on a date with him at the very least. And then there was Zoe.

The driver turned down a street and stopped in front of the building that housed Scott & Ricks. As Nick took the elevator to Adrian Scott's office for the PR meeting about the museum, he couldn't help but wonder which floor Zoe worked on and if he was losing his mind.

Zoe followed April into the elevator.

"How was your first day?"

Zoe turned so April could see her entire face. "Long, but good." Her right index finger slid partway up her left arm before she stopped herself.

"You sign?" April pointed to Zoe's hand.

"My youngest brother is deaf. We all learned, but my skills are not good." She knew her syntax was off, but other than a weekend home here and there, she hadn't signed regularly for a few years.

April's hands started flying.

Zoe only caught a few words. She signed back, "Slower, please. It has been awhile."

April slowed her signing. "No one else in the office signs other than Ms. Ricks." April spelled out the name and then used a name sign. "If you ever need to talk and don't want someone to overhear, come find me."

"I guess the same goes for you."

The elevator dinged, and they got out on the first floor. April checked her watch. "I am late to meet my boyfriend. Lunch tomorrow?"

"Sure. Later." Zoe turned in the direction of the subway stop.

"April must be thrilled to have another signer in the office."

Zoe turned at the sound of James's voice behind her. "Oh, I am sure she finds the office environment challenging. My brother is always afraid he is missing something at school." This year he started high school at the state school in Indianapolis.

They walked down the stairs. Zoe double-checked the map and directions before putting her card through the turnstile.

James stayed at her side. "By this time next week, you'll be a pro and come running through here like the rest of us."

"That obvious?"

He laughed. "Live here long enough, and you learn to distinguish the tourists from the locals pretty fast."

"So I'm a tourist?" Zoe picked a spot on the platform to wait.

"You aren't dressed tourist, but you don't act local, either. I would suggest you get a cross-body bag and carry the way she is." James pointed to a woman in front of them.

The train whooshed into the station, and they squeezed aboard with the other passengers. Zoe found a spot near a pole and held on. James grabbed an overhead bar near her. As the train started, she planted her feet.

"Yup, tourist."

James got off two stops later. Zoe kept an eye on the map, not wanting to miss her stop and connection. A mother sitting with her children on the bench in front of her used the time to quiz the older daughter on the alphabet. Most passengers stared at their phones. Doors opened and closed. The overhead sign announced the next stop. The train turned to the right. She didn't remember the turn from this morning. She studied the map again, then consulted the app on her phone. Rats! She had missed the transfer station. The next stop should put her at the bottom of Central Park. She would only need to walk a mile or so to the apartment, which was better than backtracking and finding a train going the other way.

At the top of the stairs, she tried to get her bearings as people dodged around her. Nothing looked familiar from her walk the other day. After walking two blocks and not finding the park, she turned and walked the other direction.

So many buildings were constructed of the same brick and style that using them to navigate became pointless. She turned right only to find the street numbers decreasing. She turned again. Eventually she would either run into her street or the park. As long as the street numbers went up, she could get home. However, her ankles might break from these stupid shoes first.

A car honked, and someone yelled her name.

Nick had his driver double-park long enough to hop out of the town car. He jogged back down the street. "Zoe! What are you doing over here?"

"Going home after work?" The uncertainty in her voice tugged at his heart.

Nick didn't point out that she was over a mile away and looked lost. Not the safest combination in the city. "My driver is circling the block. No offense, but those shoes are not meant to hike as far as you need to go. May I offer you a ride?"

She nodded. "Thanks for rescuing me, again."

"Let me guess. You missed your stop and figured you could just walk from the next one?" Nick steered her to a place where his driver could stop without blocking traffic.

"Pretty much. I got turned around and couldn't find the park." His driver pulled up. Nick opened the door and let Zoe slide in first. He slipped in after her and gave his driver Sean's old address. "How was your first day?"

"Overwhelming. Wonderful."

"No wonder you got lost. Were you going to text me?" Nick made a mental note to show her how to use one of the map apps to track her location.

"After leaving so ungraciously Sunday, I wasn't sure I should." She bit her lip.

"I bought Little Miss Eloise. She does make an excellent addition to my Hilary Knight mural."

"You really have a mural in your place by the author of the Eloise books?" She met his eye.

"I told you I lived where she did."

Zoe's mouth formed an O.

"You are invited anytime." He didn't expect her to take him up on the invitation.

"Maybe sometime." She looked out the window as she answered.

"Your mother taught you never to be alone in a guy's apartment with him, didn't she?"

The color in her cheeks heightened.

"It is a good rule. My mother told my sisters the same thing. If you want, you could call your cousin and have her on a video call the entire time I give you the tour, or I can get my younger sister to come over one evening. Would that work for you?" He played with one of his cuff links while he waited for her answer.

The driver found a space a couple doors down from Zoe's apartment.

"I am sure a tour with Candace would work. I'd hate to put your sister out." She slid across the seat and out the door he held open.

Not letting the opportunity to spend more time with Zoe slip by, Nick checked his watch. "How about in an hour and a half? I need to do a couple things first."

"That works." She waved and walked down the street.

Nick got back into the car.

"Sebastian, take note of this address. I have a feeling it will become familiar." He hoped. Her agreeing to see him again tonight was a huge step.

"It already is, sir. Your friend Sean's place?"

"And that is why you are the best driver in the city." He resisted the urge to text Colin to make sure Candace was free. What would Zoe think of his place? Too much? Chances were her parents' house was smaller than his penthouse. If his money was really that big of an issue to her, this would be a good test. At least his place didn't have something ostentatious like a live-in butler or helipad.

eight

ZOE DUG THROUGH HER CLOSET. Everything felt a bit too country mouse. The microwave dinged. Candace's words from yesterday's phone call came back to her. *"Nick is generous. Tessa says he always has been, and she's suspected he was behind the repaired organ pipes since Christmas. I don't think he is trying to buy you. It is just his way."*

He hadn't asked for anything in return, yet. She was still nervous about going to his penthouse with only a video call as a chaperone. She had spent most of yesterday looking him up online. If cyberspace was right, Nickolas C. Gooding was as good as his name.

She washed her fork, then tossed the plastic container away, checking it to see what she'd just eaten. She couldn't recall eating a bite.

Her phone buzzed. **We are about a block away. The driver asks if you can come down. Parking is tricky.**

Coming.

Zoe double-checked her lock before heading down.

Nick held the door open for her. "Sebastian would have gotten out, but this is faster."

Zoe slid across the seat.

"Zoe, meet Sebastian. He has been driving for me since I was in elementary school. Sebastian, this is Zoe."

Sebastian nodded in the mirror and started the car forward.

Nick turned in his seat. "Next time you are lost, please give me a call. I may not be able to find you, but Sebastian will. If I am in a meeting or something, he will get you home."

"You don't need to do that. I mean, it's a lot of trouble." She hoped she didn't come across as ungrateful.

Sebastian turned onto a busier street and caught Zoe's eye in the mirror. "I'd be happy to pick you up. I get bored waiting for this kid sometimes. It would give me something to do."

"Well, thank you for the offer. But I am not planning on getting lost again." Checking her map app after she'd gotten home, Zoe had realized the app had a locator feature. Next time, she would know where she was.

"Did you plan on getting lost tonight?" Nick adjusted his seat belt and turned to face her.

"No."

"Well, then, you never know when you might need a bit of help."

Zoe showed him her phone. "I should have realized I had this."

Sebastian made another turn and glanced in the review mirror at Zoe. "I've been driving in this city for over thirty years. GPS doesn't always tell you everything you need to know. I have seen a lot of stuff I wish I hadn't driving these streets. Please don't hesitate to call. It only takes being a block or two off from where you should be for things to go a way you don't intend."

"Are you two trying to scare me?"

Nick touched her arm. "Not much, but we do want you to call if you need to."

Sebastian pulled into an underground parking garage. "Nick, make sure you give her my direct line." He parked the car, got out, and opened Zoe's door. "And don't you hesitate to call if you need to. My only job is to drive Nick, and occasionally his family, around, so I have lots of free time." The look the driver gave her reminded Zoe so much of her father she didn't dare say anything but yes. Finding friends in the city was easier than she thought.

Over the phone, Candace oohed and aahed twice as often as Zoe. On several occasions, Zoe had to show Candace a painting or a room layout more than once. Nick left them alone to wander while he checked what goodies his housekeeper had left. Vanilla ice cream, bananas, chocolate sauce. Good banana splits pushed his cooking skills to the limit.

He followed the sound of Zoe's voice to the second floor and out to the balcony. She'd found something she admired—the park. Twilight did not do the view justice. Sometime, he would show her the park in daylight. Nick leaned against the rail next to her. "The entire principality of Monaco would fit inside the park."

"I've heard that before, but I can't picture Monaco being so small. I mean, the park is not much bigger than my father's eight-hundred-acre farm, which is on the large side but only because he bought my uncle out."

Over the phone, Candace laughed. "I hadn't thought of the size in terms of the farm, but you are right."

"So were you both raised on a farm?" The concept was something out of books like *Charlotte's Web*. He tried to picture both women with pigs and horses.

Candace answered. "We were. Zoe can detassel corn faster than any girl in the county. That's how she got crowned Corn Princess three years running." Zoe angled the phone so Nick could see Candace.

Nick would have to ask about the corn thing later.

"She made me run just so she could be Corn Princess." Zoe rolled her eyes.

He knew better than to question the existence of a corn royalty. "Don't take *stalk* in anything she says."

Zoe turned the phone. "None of your *corny* jokes."

"Fine. I'll save them for Halloween. Then they will be *early*."

"Aw, *shucks*, ladies, you two are *a-maize-ng* with the puns." Nick joined in. He wasn't the biggest punster, but he did enjoy a few.

Zoe turned and stared. "You pun?"

"Occasionally, but I have *field* my pun quota for today." He hoped the general farm one worked.

A loud groan came from the phone. "Make him stop! He is worse than you."

"Says the one who started it." Zoe glared at the phone.

They all laughed.

"If you are done with the tour, I have ice cream in the kitchen." Nick stepped back and allowed Zoe to enter the open doorway first.

Halfway down the stairs, she paused, looking at her phone. "Sure. Tomorrow." Zoe pocketed the phone and finished descending the stairs. "Candace had someone at the door and needed to go."

"Do you want to stay for ice cream? We could grab something at one of the restaurants downstairs instead."

She took a minute to weigh her decision, then looked at him for a long moment before answering. "I think I can stay long enough for ice cream."

They made their sundaes and took them out to the porch.

Zoe sat in one of the wrought-iron chairs at the table. "Do you get used to the sounds of traffic all night long?"

"I don't hear the traffic inside other than the occasional siren. So I guess I never thought about it. Are you having problems sleeping?"

"Not much. The first night I think I heard every sound. But my first summer home after going to college, I thought the silence would keep me up all night, and then the rooster started his wake-up call. I wanted to wring his neck."

"The Cottage in Blue Pines doesn't have any traffic, so I spent most of my early years there but came into the city often enough the noise never bothered me."

"So you didn't grow up in the city?"

"Not in the way Sean did. My bedroom was at the Cottage. I had one at the penthouse my dad kept here, but I didn't go to elementary school in the city. Blue Pines is home, and coming to the city was a vacation, only closer than the other places Mom and Dad took us."

"But you decided to live in the city, not in Blue Pines. Why?" Her bowl was half empty. His was almost gone.

Nick slowed his eating to prolong the conversation. "I didn't want to be one of those guys who went home after college to live with Mom and Dad. Can you see the headlines on the gossip papers? 'Rich-as-Midas trust-fund kid lives in parents' basement.' I did stay at my parents' place in the city until I found this place."

She smiled. "I think you found the perfect place. If I was to ever dream up a Plaza, this one may be beyond my imagination. Of course, I am living a dream right now. New York. Scott & Ricks. And now I am eating ice cream at Eloise's."

"With a billionaire."

"Oh yes, eating ice cream with a billionaire at Eloise's. It's like I am the star of some weird reality show where all my dreams come true."

"Even the billionaire part?" He needed to know. If the money was as huge an obstacle as she'd made it sound at the wedding, there wouldn't be much of a future for them.

"Well, since all your gold was stolen ..."

"I got most of the gold back ... though some of the platinum is rumored to have been smuggled to Canada."

She made an exaggerated thinking face. "Any dream would be incomplete without a friend, so the fact that you live in this castle can be overlooked. Thanks for rescuing me today and for inviting me up. I am sorry about my reaction to you buying a doll. I am not comfortable having money spent on me. But that is my problem, not yours."

"If you are calling me friend, then how you feel about my money is our problem." He reached over and took her fingers in his, then gave them a gentle squeeze. "Would you like me to take you home now?"

"I think so."

"Come on, then, and you can roll your eyes at my overpriced car." Nick gave her a huge smile.

She smiled back and rolled her eyes.

Progress. He'd wait for more.

nine

IT HAD TAKEN LESS THAN a week to get to the point she wasn't watching the map the entire subway ride and could walk to the correct platform without double-checking. Zoe pretended to read something interesting on her phone to blend in but still wasn't comfortable ignoring the sights and sounds of her first Friday morning commute. Her phone vibrated, and a text from Nick popped up.

—**Busy tonight? Dad was going to take Mom to a show, but she isn't feeling well. He gave me his tickets. Want to go?**

Did he mean a movie or Broadway? Not wanting to look ignorant, Zoe didn't ask. **Sure, what time?**

—**Show starts at eight. Pick you up at seven.**

Okay, see you then. :)

—**Aren't you going to ask which one?**

Does it matter? It is just part of the NYC dream.

—**LOL. To most people, yes.**

Fine, what show?

—**It's a surprise.**

FYI, I am rolling my eyes. Zoe inserted an eye-roll emoji for good measure.

55

Business people hurried down the sidewalks. Ahead of her, James waited at the door to the building. "Morning, Zoe. Ready for Friday?"

"Ready as I'll ever be. Any Friday traditions I need to know about?"

"Not that I can think of. Other than don't take off early without clearing it with Gina." James waited for the next elevator.

April joined them. "Morning."

At her desk, Zoe put her bag in the locking drawer after turning her phone to silent. Company policy didn't forbid phones in the building, but they were not allowed in certain areas due to sensitive projects, so the policy was to keep them locked away and out of sight. Use was permitted in the outer lobby and break room only. She turned on her tablet and computer. She was assigned to April this morning. There was no specific task, so Zoe made her way to April's cubicle. When she entered, she made sure she stepped on the mat that flashed a light near the monitor. April turned and signed, "Come in. Sit."

"Sign or English?" Zoe asked in both languages.

"Sign. I'll teach you signs about work."

April brought up a layout program and flipped through the pages of an annual report. Within minutes, both women were focused on the project and the morning sped by. The light flashed by the monitor. Both women turned to find Gina standing there.

"It was so quiet in here I didn't know if you were working together. I didn't know you signed, Zoe. Anyway, next Tuesday is 9/11. The firm is involved in several memorials and celebrations. One of them is out in Blue Pines. Have you ever heard of the town?"

"One of my old roommates lives there." Zoe both signed and spoke, knowing April was not at an angle where she would be able to read her lips well.

Gina nodded. "That may explain this. You have been asked to join the PR group going to the opening of a new exhibition in the museum." Gina handed Zoe an invitation.

"Tessa did a new window. She was telling us about her design last week."

Gina raised a brow. "You know Tessa Doyle Cavanagh?"

"Yes." Zoe wasn't sure if that was the wrong answer.

"She is very talented. I got to go to her studio to take some photos for the informational brochure to accompany the unveiling."

"So are you going too?" Zoe continued to sign as she spoke.

"I am. You'll need to be here a half hour earlier on the eleventh. We'll be taking a car service rather than the train." Gina nodded and left.

Zoe still could not tell if the invitation was a good or bad thing.

April waved her hand in front of Zoe's face. "I don't understand. This is a VIP event. Wayne was not happy when Gina got invited and he didn't. You are an intern. Why you?"

"Maybe because I was also Tessa's bridesmaid?"

April signed a string of words that didn't accurately translate to "Wow, you have connections," but the meaning was about the same.

"No, I have friends." Zoe couldn't help wondering which friend had orchestrated her invitation. Tessa was still on her honeymoon and probably wasn't thinking about her old roommates.

"So, will this invitation cause me problems with office politics?"

"I don't know. I am not always aware of the undercurrents. But I think Gina would be the better art director. Though Wayne's design is brilliant, he grumbles too much at the other employees. Enough. Let's finish this." April pointed to her screen.

Nick spent more time watching Zoe's expression out of the corner of his eye than he did the stage. She tried to hide her reactions to the theater, which only endeared her more to him. Her wide-eyed response to everything made him see the city—both its beauties and bruises—with new eyes. Zoe tapped her fingers in her lap as the notes of the finale played. Her hands moved as they had during some of the other musical numbers. He assumed the movements were sign language.

When the curtain fell, Zoe stood and clapped with the rest of the audience. "That was amazing."

"I noticed you have most of the songs memorized." One more thing they had in common. One woman he'd brought to *Les Mis* thought that musical theater was dumbed-down opera and said as much to anyone who would listen. She didn't even know any Italian.

"Doesn't everyone?" Zoe's eyes darted about the theater as if she were trying to memorize everything. She needn't worry. He would bring her back.

"You have a point. Were you also signing?"

"Bad habit. My brother Trey loves music, so I try to make the songs as much fun as I can. Sometimes my hands start moving on their own, and the songs from this musical are so fun."

Nick took Zoe's hand and led her out of the theater. "Do you want to go get dessert?"

"Sure."

"Should I call Sebastian, or do you want to walk?"

"We can walk. No point in bugging him yet."

They exited the theater. Nick released Zoe's hand but wished he hadn't. "Cannoli, chocolate, or ice cream?"

"I don't care." Zoe moved closer and took his arm. "Do you know you are being followed?"

He pulled his elbow in a bit, knowing but not caring who followed them. "Tall guy, early thirties, brown hair? Or shorter, late forties, and a cap?"

"How did you know?" She leaned into his side.

"I pay them to follow me." Maybe not enough.

Zoe glanced over her shoulder. "How come I have never seen them before?"

58

"They're experts, and you haven't spent that much time with me. I don't need them often. But walking around the city in a crowd could be one of those times I need them close."

Zoe grew silent but didn't let go of his arm. "Should I have chosen not to walk?"

"They were in the theater."

"Oh. I should have guessed. Abbie was Mandy Crawford's bodyguard until this summer. I got used to having someone from Hastings around all the time."

"Does having them around bother you?" He hoped it wouldn't. Having a detail came with the territory. Eventually, his wife and children would have them too.

"Not really. Having Abbie around this year has gotten me used to the concept. I can pretend they are not around. So, what are we going to get for dessert?"

Her hold on his arm relaxed. Several places over ten blocks away became dining possibilities, if only so they could walk like this. Reluctantly, Nick chose a place on the next block with to-die-for cannoli.

ten

Zoe hugged Tessa. "The window is beautiful. Thanks for making sure I had the opportunity to come to this." Sean cried openly at the unveiling of the window, as had many people in the room. The reverend added an impromptu prayer to the program, the rare type of prayer that made Zoe believe God listened and cared.

"I didn't invite you. I mean, I wish I'd thought of having you here, but with the wedding, the only thing I was worried about today was the window. Not that I needed to. Nick made sure about that. I even bugged him at the reception." Tessa turned to the crowd. "I'd better go meet some of these other people."

Zoe searched the crowd and found Nick conversing with an older couple at the other end of the hall. She recognized them as the donors of one of the paintings their daughter had completed weeks before she'd died in the terrorist attack. Zoe bit her lip. There would be no way to prove Nick had arranged for her to attend the unveiling, and even if she did, what good would it do?

The atmosphere in the office yesterday was arctic chill. April said the department was usually "cold-strange" like this after Wayne returned from one of his vacations or business trips. Other than a two-minute welcome-to-the-team speech in his office after the Monday morning meeting, she'd had no contact with the art director. Zoe searched for the other Scott & Ricks employees and found them chatting near the door.

Gina was speaking with a woman who appeared to be in her fifties and who had been introduced as the director of the public-relations arm of the firm. Zoe struggled to remember her name. They both turned to Zoe.

"Are you ready to go?" asked Gina.

Zoe nodded and followed them to the car.

"Gina told me you used to be roommates with the new Mrs. Cavanagh, and I noticed you in a couple of photos from the wedding I was given to release to the media. I assume that is why Adrian added you to the attendee group today." There was only curiosity in the woman's voice.

Zoe hoped she wasn't stepping into something political. "That is my assumption also. Although I didn't ask for it."

"The interesting thing is, as near as I can tell, it is all coincidence you are here. Adrian had no idea about the connection when he called his old friend asking for a last-minute intern recommendation." The woman took the seat on the left. Gina signaled for Zoe to sit in the middle again.

The head of PR had checked on her. Zoe stiffened. How deep would she have dug and why?

After the driver closed the door, Gina spoke. "It is more than a coincidence. I think you both being here demonstrates the caliber of your art college. Maurene, Zoe has only been with us a week, and so far she is the best new intern I have had in the past two years."

Zoe tried to hide her shock. Best in two years. It couldn't be true. All she accomplished in a week was finding some photos and listening in on meetings.

Maurene leaned forward. "I see your point about the school. Sorry if I am making you feel nervous, Zoe, but I am constantly on the lookout for things that may need to be handled later, even internally. Yesterday someone complained that a mere intern had been added to the group for the Blue Pines Museum, though the fact you attend the college Tessa Cavanagh graduated from should be enough to explain your invitation, especially since Adrian also has connections at your school."

"I didn't mean to make anyone upset." Words could get vicious when the wrong person was crossed.

"Some people get upset very easily. Don't worry about it." Gina patted her arm.

But Zoe did. If she was right about the origin of her invitation, then admitting she counted Nick Gooding among her friends might put a spin on things she didn't want to deal with. Her phone vibrated. Since the other two women were consulting their phones, Zoe decided to check the text. It was from Nick.

—Do you want to attend the 9/11 light memorial with me tonight?

Yes, but—**I am going with a friend from work.**

—K. Have a good day.

You too.

Friends was a comfortable place to be.

It had been nearly a week since he had seen Zoe, an unexpected trip to deal with hurricane cleanup having goofed up his schedule. The side trip to Chicago had been more enjoyable. Candace had reacted to the carousel like a kid with a golden ticket in a candy factory. Nick had completed his part of the plan by giving Candace a reason to be in Chicago for the next several months. The rest would be up to Colin. One Wilson woman was all Nick had the time for.

Zoe's texts and phone calls added an element of fun his life had been missing. Last night they had exchanged over fifteen pun texts that had him laughing so hard Sebastian may have questioned his sanity. Their nightly chats helped him clear his head after a long day. Zoe saw the city through new eyes, a view he hadn't experienced since he was a child—the unpleasant smells, the experience of riding the subway after years of having a driver, the way an old lady from the Bronx reacted to a friendly smile. He wished he could help her keep the Midwest friendliness that made New Yorkers look at her like she needed to be locked up in Bellevue. One just couldn't smile at old ladies on subways or laugh at children in the park you weren't related to. That was one of the nice things about Blue Pines. Zoe had solved a mystery he'd spent his entire life wondering about—namely, the answer to why his parents hadn't raised him in the city.

Nick smiled and checked his watch. Zoe wouldn't be off work for at least another hour. He texted, knowing not to expect a response soon.

The first weekend of October. There are some apple festivals upstate. Leaves are changing. Will you come enjoy them with me?

Three hours later he got his reply.

—When would we LEAF?

He smiled at the pun and struggled to come up with an apple pun in return.

Dessert at Lucinda's to discuss it?

— You are ROTTEN with the puns tonight ... Dessert sounds good. I'd like to see you.

Pick you up at 7.

— Sounds DELICIOUS.

Best place in the Big APPLE.

— Rolling eyes three to one. You must have jet lag.

Not really. Nick just couldn't think of another pun that didn't involve how appealing it was to spend part of the evening with her. And he wasn't sure she was ready for him to admit that.

eleven

THE SMALL TOWNS OF UPSTATE New York each had their own flavor—so different from the city that dominated the perception of the state. Zoe wondered which of the cars following them contained the ever-present bodyguards. Now that she knew what they looked like, she noticed them often. Occasionally one would ride with Sebastian. She had grown used to Sebastian at the wheel and not needing to pay attention to traffic for fear of interrupting the driver at a critical moment. Today Nick drove, his eclectic mix of music playing through the stereo, something he never played when they rode in the town car. The three-hour drive was the longest she had been alone with him.

Alone.

She turned the word over in her mind. In this car with this man, the word held no fear, only comfort.

When the song playing ended, Nick interrupted her musings. "You have officially spent one-twelfth of your year in New York. How do you like it?"

"I still feel a bit like the country mouse. Work is wonderful, although I still feel the art director, Wayne Dodd, is not pleased with me. Gina says the surliness is his manner." She had to agree with April—Gina would be a better art director than Mr. Dodd.

For some reason, calling him Wayne didn't work for her. It implied a closeness she didn't feel.

"Office politics. You would think I am one of the few people immune, but I have to be careful not to start something. We all bring our preconceived notions and beliefs to work with us, and where telling one person they did a good job means exactly that, another will manage to turn my words or actions into a sign I am racist or have a gender bias. Statements my father made when he was my age would put me in the crosshairs of some special-interest group if I said them today." Nick followed the instructions on a roadside sign and turned left for the festival they were going to attend.

"A month ago, I thought you had life easy, but you work harder than anyone I know. I'm really sorry for the way I treated you at the wedding."

Nick smiled but continued to look at the road. "Well, I had to work to get all my gold back."

"*Lifestyles of the Rich and Famous* didn't show the whole picture. I'm glad we are friends." Zoe savored the word. She had a friend who was a man. Not that she was ready to put the thought together in one word, but for the first time in two years, the idea that she could have a friend who was a guy didn't send her into hiding.

"Me too." He gave her a quick smile before focusing on a curve in the road.

Below them, a valley opened, along with a vista of greens, yellows, and oranges. Zoe blinked. The view was stock-photo worthy. "Don't tell the Indiana Department of Tourism, but New York leaves blow their ads away."

Nick chuckled. "As a New Yorker, I shouldn't say this, but Vermont and New Hampshire probably win."

"My old roommate Araceli is from Boston, and she said the same thing every fall whenever the ad for Indiana ran on TV."

Nick found a parking space. Zoe reached for the handle of her door, but he stopped her with a hand on her arm. "We need to wait a moment for security to get into place since there is a crowd. Also, what would my mother say if I didn't get your door?"

He didn't remove his hand. She didn't want him to. "I don't know your mother very well. What would she say?"

Nick furrowed his brow. "I'm not entirely sure, but I think she might include the words *uncouth* and *Neanderthal*."

"I wouldn't want her to lecture you. I'll wait."

Nick's phone beeped. He exited the car and opened Zoe's door with a flourish that would make his mother proud. Zoe inhaled deeply. The air smelled of apples and cinnamon. "I think I found a bit of heaven. I hope they have applesauce donuts and caramel-apple cider."

"Deep-fried pies are my favorite. Why don't we get something now, and then we can eat more before we go?" They set off down one of the rows of vendor tents.

Apple sausage, apple crisp, apple hash, apple salad, apple-and-ham sandwiches, apple dumplings, caramel apples ... "How can I choose? There are so many options."

"I'm going to start with something that has protein, like the apple ice cream, so I can pretend I had a balanced diet."

Zoe side bumped him. "I don't think that is very balanced."

"Well, I will try some games for exercise after, like the bushel lift and apple bobbing."

The day was filled with laughter fueled by too much sugar. When Nick attempted the apple bob, his bodyguards moved closer than they had all day. His head came up flinging water everywhere, a MacIntosh gripped firmly in his teeth—his shirt plastered to his upper torso. Zoe's breath caught. Under the suits, she had never noticed the muscles. She looked away before he found her blushing.

She tried to catch the apple hanging from a string. It was difficult to do when Nick was cheering her on and she was focused on his damp shirt. On the third attempt, she succeeded. The smell of cinnamon must be some love potion invented by a benevolent witch. That would explain away her new awareness. Not entirely new. She'd ignored the current at the wedding, but the acknowledgment was as fresh as the hot donuts they ate. Maybe the apples contained the magic. After all, Eve had eaten an apple.

They window-shopped in the craft and vendor booths. Everything from pens to platters was available in an apple theme.

Zoe picked up a rag doll. "Isn't she cute?" Red yarn hair topped the doll's freckled, embroidered head. Her calico pinafore was sprinkled with apples, and an embroidered red delicious covered the spot where the doll's heart should be.

"Quite a-*peel*ing."

"Are you going *hard-core* on the puns?"

"Maybe, or it could be an in-*cider* joke?" He stepped closer.

Zoe set the doll down. "Oh, I—" She couldn't think about apples when Nick was in her space and she wanted him to stay there. "I have nothing."

"Then I win and get my *apply*-ever after."

Zoe picked up the doll again, mostly so she wouldn't concentrate on Nick. "That was *rotten*."

"Don't be a *crab*."

Zoe turned to Nick. "Fine, you won this round. What is your prize?"

Nick looked her in the eye, then dropped his gaze to her mouth. Zoe's heart raced. His gaze returned to her eyes. "I'd like to buy you something apple-ish to remember the day."

Zoe lifted the doll higher. "She is pretty cute."

Nick's fingers brushed hers when he took the doll from her hands, and they both froze. Around them, people laughed, talked, and ate, but for Zoe, not even the bodyguards watching them registered at that moment. Zoe released the doll.

"Shall I get her for you?"

Not sure if she could find her voice, she nodded.

Someplace north of Poughkeepsie, Zoe fell asleep clutching the doll he'd bought her. Nick yawned and wished he didn't have to drive the rest of the way into Manhattan. The clock on the dash read 10:15. Blue Pines was closer. Nick pushed the Talk button on his steering wheel three times.

"Yes, Mr. Gooding?" one of the bodyguards answered.

"I am starting to fall asleep. Do you know if the detail roster has my parents at the Cottage this weekend?"

"Just a moment, and we will check."

Nick waited until the bodyguard came back on. "Yes, they are, as well as your sister."

"Change of plans. We are heading there."

"Do you need to pull over and have one of us drive?"

"No, I can stay awake for another thirty minutes. If I think I am falling asleep, I'll let you know."

"We will be watching your tail. The first time you swerve, we will ask you to pull over."

"Fair enough. Later." Nick pressed the Talk button again and instructed the phone to call his mother.

"Long time, Nick. What do you need?"

"I'm driving back from the apple festival, and I don't think I'll stay awake for the rest of the drive into the city. Mind if I crash?"

"You are always welcome, and you never need call."

"I have a friend with me, one of Tessa's bridesmaids. I'd call Sean, but …"

"I'll have a room made up for her. Don't bug Sean. He is still honeymooning."

"Thanks, Mom."

"Drive safe."

Zoe woke up as they exited the freeway. "Where are we?"

"This is the exit for Blue Pines. I am too tired to drive the rest of the way. My parents and sister are at the house. I called Mom, and she will have a room ready for you. If you prefer, I can get you a hotel."

Zoe covered a yawn. "Your parents are home. I think the house is fine."

He should have prepared her. The house he called his residence was not a mere house. He turned into the drive and pulled up to the gate, which opened automatically. Then he drove up the lane.

Zoe gasped. "That is *not* a house. That is bigger than the old Crawford mansion!"

"My great-grandmother called it a cottage. In fact, the property is named the Cottage, but I usually think of it as home."

"You are kidding me. What was her other home—a castle?"

Nick shifted uncomfortably. "As a matter of fact, it was. She was the third daughter of a prince of a small European country."

"Oh. So you are a prince?" There was a teasing tone in her voice.

"No, she became an American citizen before World War I and renounced her place in the monarchy."

"According to my mother, my genealogy ties into British royalty—only, my ancestors renounced their country before the Revolution."

Nick parked in front of the house. "So you are a princess. That explains a lot." Before she reach for the handle, he exited the car and raced around to open her door. "Welcome to the Cottage, princess."

Zoe rolled her eyes. Or he thought she did. It was hard to tell under the exterior lighting.

Nick took her hand and led her into the front foyer, aware that he was sending an obvious statement to his family about his intentions, even if Zoe didn't recognize the significance of her presence at the Cottage.

Zoe reached for her phone to hit the snooze. She was beginning to see why people hated Mondays. She wanted to dream of her weekend again. Not that her dreams could improve on the

Cottage. Nick's parents hadn't made her feel uncomfortable with invasive questions like she expected, and his sister had loaned her a set of still-packaged pajamas. If it were not for the size of the Cottage, she would have thought she was with any of her friends' families back home. They had even attended church, Zoe in borrowed clothes, as a family. The unplanned meeting of the family did not produce the cliché set of nerves.

Her phone beeped. Zoe sat up to answer the text. Candace. **Didn't hear from you this weekend. Tessa said she saw you at church. What's up?**

We went to an apple festival and stopped at Nick's parents' for the night. Not much.

—So, was THIS one a date?

The question was certainly valid. Until now, the shows, desserts, and even a football game party at his penthouse with some of his friends had been classified under the heading of hanging out.

It may have been. I know I said I didn't want to date him because of his money. But he is a nice person. I think I can trust him. He offered to put me in a hotel if I wasn't comfortable with staying with his family. How was your weekend?

—Good. I went to the house. Colin came (but stayed at Crawfords').

So, was THAT a date? Zoe tossed off her covers and started her morning routine.

—Maybe.

I think we both went on dates and don't want to admit it.

—Probably. I think I need another ten-year plan. Dr. told me I can make a fifty-year one.

I don't think I could plan for fifty, but it is nice knowing you can. Gotta run, or I'll be late.

—Hugs!

Ditto

When she got out of the shower, there were two texts from Nick, four minutes apart.

—May I include you in my Wednesday-night plans?

—Are you awake? It's Monday. Come on, sleepyhead.

I'm awake. Farm girl, remember? She wouldn't admit she was running late.

—Tuesday?

I thought you said Wednesday.

—That too.

What kind of plans?

—I don't know yet.

Zoe's heart pounded. No mistaking this would be a date. Her thumb hovered over the *N* for a moment, but the apple doll smiled up at her from the dresser, urging her to take a chance.

Waiting for Zoe's text was worse than waiting for the note in third grade to make its way back from the front of the classroom. Check yes or no.

—Yes, please include me both nights. Any ideas?

One or two.

—Like what?

I'll let you know.

—That is mean to do to a girl who must turn off her phone for most of the day.

Sorry.

—You are smiling, aren't you?

Only if you are rolling your eyes.

She sent an eye-roll emoji. He returned a big grin emoji before stepping into the elevator.

Sebastian met him at the car. "Good morning. I haven't seen you smile that big on a Monday morning since the last stock split."

Nick handed his driver a bag of spiced, dried apples. "I believe you said you liked these."

"So, did you take anyone up with you this year?" Judging from the grin Sebastian wore, he knew the answer and that the trip to the festival had included a day at the Cottage.

Nick got in the back seat, positive Sebastian would know from the security reports. "Are you going to stand around talking all day? I'll be late to work."

Sebastian got in his seat. "I'd never make you late." He smiled in the rearview mirror. "I wanted to know if I would get to see Miss Wilson again."

"Tomorrow night." Nick checked to make sure his cuff links were straight. He had a habit of playing with them when he was nervous. He noticed he'd been fiddling with them more since Sean's wedding.

As Sebastian pulled into Monday morning traffic, Nick replayed his favorite moments from the weekend: The seconds when the world had stopped as Zoe handed him the rag doll. Kaylee and Zoe laughing about him—he was sure about that—on the back patio after lunch. Zoe's blush when they said good night. He would have kissed her, but the fact that Mrs. Clark was watching from her window stopped him.

He wondered if he would see Zoe tonight as well.

twelve

IN MID-OCTOBER, ZOE BOARDED THE subway, no longer feeling like a wide-eyed country mouse. As she took her place next to a pole and read the morning news on her phone, her mind wandered over the past week and a half. The week following the apple festival, a new routine had started for Zoe—a quick text chat with Nick in the morning and a line or two during her lunch break. Some evenings they met for dinner, but others they only talked on the phone as either one of her projects would keep her late or Nick would have some business-related function.

He hadn't invited her to any of those yet. Zoe didn't mind, as often the paparazzi was in attendance at the charity and political dinners and she was not ready to make a public statement about their dating. Publicity was one of the things she'd discussed with Nick. Knowing Mandy's experience, Zoe was jumpy about the subject. Caught too often in photographs together, and someone would start invading her privacy. It wouldn't take much to dig up the skeletons she wanted to remain buried.

Friday night's date had included catching a movie at the refurbished Blue Pine's theater, which specialized in old classics with an organist playing at intermission. Saturday's had been touring Sean and Tessa's new place. At a quarter of the size of the Cottage, the house was still huge. The bare walls and rooms would be filled as they moved in.

There had been a couple moments when she wondered if Nick would kiss her and, more important, if she would kiss him back. The first kiss had been a line in their relationship they'd both danced around. She had never told him why kissing was a line for her and was left to guess with him. But she had learned from blogs and articles on the web that whenever he dated, he avoided portraying the billionaire playboy. There had even been an interviewer who'd asked him if he ever kissed on the first date. She liked his answer. "I'm not the kiss-and-tell type, but somewhere around the tenth date, we will have shared a kiss." The reporter had called him "Gooding Two Shoes," but the moniker hadn't stuck. After meeting Nick's parents, she better understood his values. The only real difference between their families was the income each generated. Ansley Gooding worked farmer's hours too.

Depending on how one counted it, they had moved beyond the tenth date. She wondered if she'd unconsciously sent out some signal warning him off. It was normal to have her heart race before a kiss. Maybe she turned away too quickly, afraid she would relive past memories. But the nightmares hadn't bothered her at all since she started ending her day with a good-night text or call to him. Next time he looked at her like he wanted to kiss her, she would meet him halfway. More, if possible.

When the overhead voice speaker announced the next station was hers, Zoe closed the app and put her phone away just seconds before the doors whooshed open. Work was becoming a comfortable routine too. Although most of her work was still supportive in nature, Gina had assigned her a couple of comprehensive layouts to do for client proposals. All of them had been for pro-bono charity clients, but the thrill of designing something rather than completing someone else's design was enough to make her stay late more than once.

April met her at the elevator. "You look tired. Did you work late again last night?"

Zoe signed back her answer. "No, I was up too late doing stuff."

"Mystery boyfriend?"

"No, my cousin called, and we talked forever. And I am not sure he is my boyfriend."

"You text every lunch, talk every night, and go out. You started buying cute new clothes." April pointed to Zoe's new blouse. "He is your boyfriend."

Zoe hoped no one else in the silent elevator understood sign. She changed the subject as they got off the elevator. "What are you working on today?"

"I don't know. WD," she used Mr. Dodd's name sign, "called a meeting this morning for some of us. Must be a big project. He usually waits until Monday. You were on the list."

"Maybe we both get something new." Zoe waved as they split off to their own cubicles.

James stood near hers with an insulated cup. "Thursday morning caramel cider."

Zoe hung her coat on a hook. "What do you need me to do?"

"What? I can't get you a drink out of kindness?"

She put her bag and phone in her bottom drawer. "I'm not sure. So far they have all been bribes." She took the drink and gave James a smile. Being the lowest rung on the office ladder, Zoe had no illusions as to her place.

James pulled out the color comp of a brochure. "The client doesn't like the photos they marked in red. Can you find me three alternatives for each that fit into the current crops?"

Opening her tablet's calendar, Zoe checked her schedule. "I don't have anything until a ten o'clock with Mr. Dodd. I can give you an hour."

"Thanks, Zoe."

She sipped her cider. "As long as you know how to bribe me."

Three meetings down. If he could find a way to eliminate meetings, Nick would be a trillionaire, not to mention the most famous man alive. He hoped Zoe would have her lunch break before Sebastian arrived at Nick's lunch-meeting location. He started off the thread. **Three meetings so far today. The vital part could have been handled in thirty-five minutes, total.**

Three stoplights later, Zoe responded.

—I got to participate in my first brainstorming session for a new client. Mr. D is forming a team.

Will you be on it?

—I wish. But probably not.

Why not?

—I'm the office gofer and grunt. Too big of a client. But I liked the brainstorming meeting.

Anything else interesting?

—James has learned caramel cider will put him at the top of my list of people to do grunt work for.

A second text came before he could reply.

—April says that's wrong. She is at the top of my list.

LOL. Don't tell James about the bread pudding or applesauce donuts.

—-Never. TTFN.

Have a good afternoon.

Sebastian pulled up in front of the building for the next meeting. Nick double-checked his calendar and the agenda he'd received via email. At least this meeting was to culminate in a vote rather than rehash old discussions.

An hour and fifteen minutes later, a doorman held the door open for Nick to get back in the car.

"Sebastian, I'll pay you a $10,000 bonus if you get into a fender bender so I miss the next meeting."

His driver laughed and pulled into traffic. "Your mother pays me ten times that to keep you out of accidents. I am not giving up my good-driver bonus to keep you out of another meeting."

"Fine. Will you take the most-likely-to-make-me-delayed route?"

"That I can do."

Nick sat back. Mid-October meetings were the worst. Budgets were either over or under target, and tempers ran hot. Half the boards he sat on rarely listened to him as they felt he was too young. He must have been asked three times in the last meeting why his father wasn't there. And the entire time, he thought of sharing a bread pudding with Zoe. He hadn't ever shared his food with a date, but Zoe had pointed out that they both ended up taking half of their meal home each time and food wasn't nearly as good warmed up as it was fresh. There was something intimate about getting down to the last bite of a shared dessert and the inevitable no-you-eat-it argument. Nick texted Zoe.

Bread pudding tonight?

He didn't wait for an answer. It would be after five thirty when she read it.

thirteen

AT SIX THIRTY, APRIL TAPPED Zoe on the shoulder. Out loud she said, "See you tomorrow. Have a good night." She signed, "You are the only one here. Go home."

Zoe pointed to her screen and signed, "Five minutes. Gina needs this emailed before seven for her meeting in LA."

April bit her lip and looked at her watch. "Fine, but text me later."

Speaking, Zoe said. "You too. Good night."

At the end of the hallway, the elevator dinged. Zoe opened her personal drawer and grabbed her phone. Company policy or not, she felt safer with the phone in her pocket.

Five minutes turned into ten as she added a point of leading here and changed the tracking there. Deciding she didn't dare wait any longer, she uploaded the file to the company cloud and sent an email to Gina attaching a JPEG copy of the final layout. She only had to wait a moment before she received a confirmation email with two words. "Good work."

Zoe shut down her computer and gathered her things. As she passed Mr. Dodd's office, he called out. "Night, Zoe."

Covering her racing heart with her hand, Zoe choked out, "I was just leaving."

"Did I scare you?" He pushed back from his desk, the picture of his family from a recent vacation perched on a stack of papers wobbling with the motion.

"I didn't realize anyone else was here."

Mr. Dodd held up a catalog from the shoe company they were pitching to next week. "I'm working on the team project for the new athletic-shoe account and trying to decide if you should be on it." He stood and came around the desk, then leaned on the front side. "Do you have a moment?"

She took one step inside the door.

"In today's meeting, you didn't seem to agree with James's take on the campaign. Would you mind telling me your thoughts?"

She took a deep breath, not sure her initial ideas were relevant. "Every shoe company sponsors some athlete. Don't get me wrong—I think Olympians are cool, but they aren't obtainable. What about shoes holding up to real life? Running to catch a train, playing soccer with the kids, strolling in the park with a significant other, not running the 400-meter."

He nodded. "I like it. Add them to the board." He waved his arm at the whiteboard covering the entire side wall of his office.

Zoe set her bag down on a chair and chose a purple pen from the basket. Halfway through the second-idea map, Mr. Dodd moved from the leaning against the desk to stand behind her. Zoe reached up to an empty spot and started writing. *Walking in a p—*

He moved closer, his hand settling on her back, below her waistline. "Do you walk in the park with a boyfriend?"

Zoe froze. Images of a different man, a different place, filled her head. The smell of soy nuts wafted against her cheek. She hated soy nuts. They weren't real. His hand moved lower as he took a step closer and wrapped his other arm around her front. No! This was not happening. She was stronger now. Smarter. Her voice came back strong. "Remove your hands."

He pulled her back into his chest. "Aren't you a team player? Don't you want the shoe campaign in your portfolio?"

Her months of training at the little makeshift gym at the end of the strip mall kicked in. She spun around quickly, using the pen as a weapon to slash at his face, a purple line marring him nose to ear. He swore and shoved her against the board, pinning her, his mouth grabbing hers. Soy nuts and slime. Zoe bit down at the same time she shoved the pen into his side. He leaped back far enough for Zoe to scream "No!" as she slammed her foot on his instep and brought her pen hand up to his face with enough force to knock his chin back. His hand yanked on her new blouse. Buttons flew and fabric ripped.

"Ki-ah!" Zoe aimed for his knee as he spouted off a string of expletives and lunged for her. She put all the power she had behind the next two moves.

Mr. Dodd doubled over, adding new expletives to his tirade. Blood gushed from his nose.

Zoe ran for the elevator. She pushed the buttons, but the floor indicator showed the elevator was ten floors above. Behind her, Mr. Dodd yelled. She ran around the corner to the stairway. She hit the release bar, the sound echoing loudly in the empty stairwell. Nausea rose as she looked down the stairwell. Twenty-seven floors. She'd never make it, even if she ditched the heels. Across the hall, a door stood ajar, a yellow custodian's cart next to it. Zoe dove for the door and shut it behind her, throwing the lock. The closet smelled of fake pine and lemon—cleaners that couldn't even begin to remove the filth that clung to her. Leaning back against a shelf full of toilet paper, Zoe tried to catch her breath. How long until he realized where she was and found a key? Or the custodian came back. She pulled out her phone. Should she dial 911? Or building security? She swiped the unlock code. An unanswered text from Nick sat at the top of her screen. He would know what to do, and she wouldn't need to risk talking.

Help! Trapped in the custodial closet, 27th floor.
—Call?
NO!

Footsteps pounded down the hall.

He will hear!

Her boss was close now, his yells echoing from the stairwell. Zoe assessed the closet for a weapon even as she prayed he would go down the stairs.

—Security is on their way up.

K

—Who will hear?

Mr. Dodd

The doorknob rattled. "Zoe!" yelled her boss.

Hury! She didn't care about the misspelled word. She didn't have time. Only now did she realize that her boss would be between her and all methods of escape.

—Sebastian and I are a block away.

Zoe put her phone in her pocket and grabbed a bottle of cleaner, unscrewing the lid. This time she would defend herself with every resource she could find, but in the back of her mind, she knew how far that could go. She prayed someone would get there before—

"I know you are in there!" A key scraped inside the lock.

The elevator pinged, and her phone vibrated.

Angry voices.

She gripped the bottle tighter.

The lock popped, but the door remained closed.

Mr. Dodd yelled more expletives. "She attacked me!"

"Zoe!"

At the sound of Nick's voice, she released the breath she had been holding and dropped the bottle, splashing her pants with pine-scented cleaner.

The doorknob turned. "Zoe? It's Nick. You are safe now."

He held out his hand, but she bypassed it, diving into his arms instead. They closed around her. Cinnamon and sandalwood aftershave. He kept talking, but she couldn't hear over the thought that she was safe.

"You're safe. You're safe …" Nick repeated the words. Sobs shook Zoe as she pressed farther into his arms. The elevator pinged behind him. The newcomers identified themselves as the police. He held her tighter, hoping to give her strength for what would come next. He'd watched enough TV shows to know that talking about what had just happened would be hard.

Mr. Dodd continued to shout. Nick wished he could cover his ears as well as Zoe's. The man was vile.

Someone tapped him on the shoulder. "Sir, I'm Detective Anderson." A dark-haired female showed him a badge. "I need to speak to the victim."

Nick eased his hold on Zoe and coaxed her to do likewise. Zoe's hair hung askew, half out of her bun. Her pale-pink blouse was torn, and buttons were missing. Nick slipped off his coat and draped it around Zoe's shoulders before stepping back and allowing the detective access.

"Miss? I'm Detective Anderson," the woman repeated herself. Zoe nodded. The officer turned to Nick. "Name, please?"

"Nick Gooding. This is Zoe Wilson."

The detective's eyes widened for a fraction of a second when he said his name. "Mr. Gooding, if you will speak to one of my fellow officers. Miss Wilson and I will find a better place to talk."

"There is a lounge area on the other side of the wall, or if Zoe prefers, there is a windowless boardroom the next floor up you can use."

Detective Anderson narrowed her gaze. "You can give me access to this how?"

"I own the building. By the way, I had my assistant put a call in to Adrian Scott. Either he or Shayne Ricks should be here soon." Nick didn't back down at the detective's glare.

The detective turned back to Zoe and spoke in low tones. A man stepped into Nick's line of vision and stuck out his hand.

"I'm Detective Francis. Will you step over here and answer a few questions?" Although phrased as a question, Nick had no option. He watched as Detective Anderson walked Zoe back into the office area.

"How did your driver come to be the one to call this in?"

Nick spent the next ten minutes answering questions. When the officers listened to the 911 call, they would hear his voice as well as Sebastian's. It had been dumb luck, or divine intervention, that the last meeting had run over by an hour, or he would have already been uptown. For once he was grateful for a long, boring meeting.

Mr. Dodd continued to yell even as a uniformed officer read him his rights. Too bad the right to remain silent wasn't a demand. Adrian joined Nick and the detective and volunteered video from the hallway cameras. The detective accompanied Adrian upstairs.

Nick leaned against the wall, trying to plan what he should do next but found he was clueless. A uniformed officer came over. "Mr. Gooding, Detective Anderson would like to see you." The officer showed him back to the lobby area. Zoe sat at one end of a designer couch. The detective stood to meet him before he could reach Zoe's side.

"She says you will give her a ride home. Is that correct?"

"If she wants, yes."

"She is free to go. Her bag and coat are in Mr. Dodd's office. As soon as they are done photographing, she can take them. It should be just a moment." The detective left.

Nick crouched down in front of the sofa. "Zoe?"

She looked up with tears in her eyes, her arms wrapped around her waist and holding his coat in place.

Helplessness flooded Nick. Money wouldn't help. The district attorney would handle the case. His bodyguards, who no doubt were mingling with building security and police on the other side of the wall, couldn't rewind time and take down Dodd before.

All he had to offer was what comfort she would accept. "What can I do?"

"Make sure he never comes near me again. Next time I won't go so easy on him, and I don't want to be responsible for his death." He was not prepared for the venom in her voice.

"I doubt he will be able to work in this city after his trial." It wasn't much, but it was all he had to offer.

Zoe shuddered.

The uniformed officer reappeared. "Miss Wilson, if you would like to get your bag, you may do so now."

She wiped her eyes with tissues and stood. Nick followed her and the officer down the hall. After seeing Mr. Dodd's scarred face, he expected the office to have sustained more damage. Zoe didn't look at the smeared whiteboard or the scattered papers from the end of the desk. She simply grabbed her bag and coat and shot back out of the room. Nick took another moment to assess the damage. On top of the papers lay a broken picture frame surrounding a smiling family. The man had ruined more than one life tonight.

Sebastian stood next to Zoe where she spoke to Adrian. They all looked up at his approach.

With a low voice, Adrian Scott filled Nick in. "I told Zoe Mr. Dodd is no longer in our employ." Then he turned back to Zoe. "I am deeply sorry this happened. I'll call Gina tonight. Since she is in LA, tomorrow I'll come down to the graphics department and we will have a meeting. HR will be available then. There is only one complaint in Dodd's file for verbal sexual harassment several months ago, for which he took a mandatory sensitivity class. The last intern left abruptly but claimed her departure was because of an issue at home, but I wonder if everything got reported." He turned to Zoe. "If you want the day off or need any off in the future because of what happened tonight, I'll authorize paid leave. Also, our insurance covers counseling at 100 percent."

"Thank you, Mr. Scott. I'll think about coming to work in the morning. I know I'll need to face everyone, but it might be easier after the initial announcement has been made."

Adrian nodded. "And, Zoe—" He waited until she focused on him. "You have talent. Gina has sent me more than one report of how pleased she is with your work. Don't let him ruin your career or your life. By the way, the purple marker was a nice artistic touch." Adrian's face betrayed no emotion.

The elevator opened. Sebastian held the door while Nick and Zoe entered. When the doors closed, his driver spoke. "My wife and I have an extra room if you would rather not be alone tonight."

"Thanks, Sebastian, I'll be fine. I don't need to put you out."

"It wouldn't be putting us out."

Zoe shook her head. Nick's coat swallowed her up. At some point, she had buttoned the top button. He had only been vaguely aware there was a button near the collar of his cashmere top coat. The effect made her look smaller and more vulnerable than she was. He longed to hold her but was unsure how she would take the contact as she'd kept her arms wrapped around her middle. Nick slid closer. Zoe didn't move. She didn't even seem entirely aware of him. He might not know what to do, but he knew one thing not to. Zoe should not go home alone, at least not yet. He racked his brain for anything else he could do. His money couldn't solve this. He couldn't solve this. But he would still try.

When they reached the first level of the parking garage, Sebastian held open the car door for Zoe. Nick walked around to the far side. Sebastian caught his eye and zigzagged his finger in the air. Nick nodded in agreement and got in the back seat, glad his driver had the same idea.

fourteen

HEADLIGHTS.
STOREFRONTS.
STREETLIGHTS.

The coat smelled like Nick. Cinnamon and sandalwood. It smelled like safety.

Zoe took a deep breath. She could almost taste the cinnamon. How long had she been in the back of the car? She felt her soul coming back from where it had fled. Buildings came into focus. Her hand hurt. She must have bruised it during the fight. Her shoulder did too. The taste of soy nuts still lingered.

"Gum?" Her voice sounded distant. She tried again. "Do you have any gum, please?"

"It's in the right pocket of the coat you are wearing." Nick didn't touch her as he pointed.

She pulled out a glove, then the gum. The cinnamon burned her mouth, incinerating the flavor of soy nuts. Words she'd had to force out to the detective faded. Memories of other interviews and of other questions hovered, waiting to pounce, but Nick's gum fought them back. For now, she was safe in the back of a town car. "Thank you for coming and everything."

Next to her, Nick shifted in his seat. "I'm glad you called. Building security got there just as he was trying to unlock the door. If you had called 911—"

"I had a bottle of cleaner I was going to throw in his face. I am glad I didn't have to. I keep seeing the picture of his family on the desk. I don't think I could have faced them if I had maimed him or struck a killing blow." She hadn't thought about which moves to use, just reacted, but that was the purpose of all her hours at the gym. Never again meant never again. The clearest memory she had of the fight was seeing the family photo fall from the table. Other memories would come later, or not. This time she wouldn't hide from them.

"Hungry?"

Zoe ran her hand over his coat. "I'm not exactly dressed to go out."

"I wear that cashmere coat all the time. Are you telling me I shouldn't?" Nick's teasing tone nearly coaxed a smile from her. "But I asked if you are hungry. Every other restaurant has take-out. We can eat in the car."

"I should be. I think if I had food I would eat it." Would it stay down was another question.

"I didn't get dinner either. Do you mind if I order for you?"

She nodded and looked out the window. Sebastian had found a street she didn't recognize. He was driving around to give her time. She wouldn't protest. She didn't want to go back to the apartment, where old and new nightmares awaited her. When Nick finished tapping an order into his phone, she felt he was watching and waiting for her to say something more, but she didn't look his direction. She wasn't ready for more words, and she wasn't brave enough to ask for another hug.

Sebastian circled the block. When the heated seat grew too warm, Zoe turned down her control, and as she unbuttoned the top button of the coat, Nick took a sudden interest in the world outside his window.

She reached out and touched his arm. "The detective took my shirt for evidence. I have on a shirt the EMT pulled from someplace. I may be mismatched, but I am dressed."

Nick turned to look at her. "Not mismatched. Your black skirt accents the heather gray of the shirt, but the neon logo ..." He hung his head in mock shame.

The car stopped, and Sebastian ran into a restaurant.

The logo *was* poorly designed. But after tonight, she would never see the shirt again. Sebastian opened Nick's door and handed in three food bags. Her stomach rumbled. Something inside one of them smelled edible.

"I ordered a few of your favorites."

Tonight, she wasn't going to chide him about spending too much money on her. "Fries?"

"And a shake—chocolate, with raspberries and marshmallows. I believe that's what you said your favorite was during one of our late-night phone calls. The restaurant did text me back about that combination to make sure the shake order wasn't a typo." Nick handed her the fries and set the drink in the console. "There is also a cheeseburger, extra pickle, no onion, and three kinds of brownies. If you'd rather, there is also soup and their famous rolls."

"I hope you got yourself something, too." Zoe searched through the bags for a spoon.

"I got the salad."

She stopped her search through the bag and turned to look at him.

Nick grinned and saluted her with his burger. "It's on a bun and came with beef."

Zoe ate a spoonful of the shake. The flavors matched every happy memory of her teen years hanging out at the Shake Shack with her brothers. This wasn't two years ago. She wasn't alone, and the food was going to stay down. "I think I can go back to the apartment now."

Nick hoped Zoe had a more restful night than he did. Formerly faceless stories told in meetings with lawyers and company heads now had a face. Over the last few months, he and his father had dropped a handful of investments from their portfolios because of hostile corporate climates that refused to change their harassment policies. They also donated anonymously to lawyers willing to fight cases for women who had given up hope. His father had pushed for changes in a couple of the hospitals where he sat on the board. Each story took on the terrified face of Zoe when he opened the closet—stories he'd scarcely believed rang with truth.

Nick wasn't naïve. He knew of men in his social group who used their money to influence their relationships with women. To be honest, he knew a few women who did the same. These types who saw others as stepping stones or personal entertainment—perhaps they didn't have mothers like his or a good dose of Reverend Cavanagh growing up. Maybe they believed money could buy happiness and thought happiness was something other than work, or that power and coercion were synonymous. Until last night, everything had been statistics he'd tried to change in policy and in practice, but never in person.

Every moment from the frantic seconds when he'd seen Zoe's first text replayed in his mind. Only the fact he had been on the phone with his assistant made it possible for building security to be alerted so quickly. Sebastian had dialed the hands-free phone into the 911 call center, allowing Nick to give them information while the driver had used his thirty years of Manhattan driving skills to get them to the building in record time. If they had hit another red light or been farther away, by the time he had gotten to Zoe, she could have been ... he didn't want to think about it. His nightmares detailed the statistics and stories for him.

Nick overrode the timer on the coffee pot. By 4:35 a.m. he knew he wouldn't get any more sleep. He paced the first floor while he waited, going over the day's schedule and wondering what could be rescheduled. Zoe had been unsure about going to work by the time he'd walked her to her door. If she wanted to talk, or anything else, like take him up on his offer to fly her to Indiana for the rest of the weekend, he wanted to be available. The proposal to fly her home on a private jet was the only thing that had gotten her to give him the you-spend-too-much-money-on-me look last night. Part of the reason he'd offered was to see if she would give him the eye roll. She had. Not a full one, but enough that he could leave her.

If she hadn't, he would have had Sebastian drive around all night if necessary.

He walked past his coat. The ketchup stain would be gone within hours of having the coat sent to the cleaner, but the red condiment had upset Zoe more than it should have. She insisted on paying the bill, another sign that the zombie version of Zoe that had left the office building was retreating. Nick lied. There was no way he would send the bill to her. He was only too grateful the stain was only ketchup and not her blood. He'd always known money couldn't buy everything, and last night not a single thing he wanted could be bartered for his billions. Zoe safe and smiling—he would have traded it all just for her to smile, roll her eyes at him, and laugh when he called her on it.

The timer on his coffee maker buzzed. Nick ignored it, opting for a shower instead. As soon as she would allow him, Nick wanted to be back at Zoe's side.

fifteen

ZOE'S PHONE PLAYED HER WAKE-UP song. Zoe struggled to turn the alarm off without getting paint on the screen. Sometime in the night, she'd given up on sleep. The old nightmares had mingled with the new one, and her mind had gone into overdrive. It was too early to call or text anyone. By the time she had gotten home, April had texted a dozen times. Zoe answered: **Home safe. Long story. Sorry you worried.** She needed to text a more detailed version before April got to the office. She wished she could call April like she had Mom and Candace. Signing the story over video would be worse than texting words. In print was easier to distance oneself from a subject. ASL used too many facial expressions, and the action words would be too close to what happened.

Zoe pulled off her plastic gloves. April deserved to know before she got to the office.

There was an incident last night. When I was leaving, Mr. D was still there. He called me into his office. He forcefully kissed me and wanted more. I hit him. The story is longer. I don't really want to tell it. The police took him away. Mr. Scott has already fired him.

Fifteen minutes later, April answered.

—Mr. D??? I don't want to believe it. I saw him come in as I left. I thought good, you won't be alone. You lie.

Zoe squashed the tears. She knew Deaf culture tended to be blunt, but it was hard to tell in text. At least she didn't have to be upset that the vague warnings April had given regarding staying late meant April suspected Mr. Dodd.

No. I would not have broken his nose if he had only said good night.

—Oh, it is so hard to believe. He was so nice to me.

I know it is hard to believe. Mr. Scott is having a meeting with everyone this morning.

—Are you coming to work?

Zoe had vacillated all night about what she was going to do today. Now, with her closest workplace friend not believing her, she didn't know if she could listen to the innuendo and comments of her coworkers. Thanks to the detectives, there was enough evidence for some type of assault charge, but that didn't mean Mr. Dodd would plead guilty, or the judge would listen, or her coworkers would side with her. In some ways, not being believed was worse than being assaulted.

Mr. Scott told me I could take the day off. I'll see you Monday.

By Monday she would know if she was strong enough to go back. Strong enough to not let her dream job become another nightmare.

By 7:00 a.m., Nick had finished all the work not requiring his presence in an office. Hopefully, his father would agree to cover the two meetings scheduled for the day without Nick's presence. His PA could move everything else to next week. Before he contacted either of them, he texted Zoe. **How are you this morning?**

She answered with a photo of her half-painted kitchen.

Did you sleep at all?

—Not much. I am not going in today. April didn't believe me, so I am a coward.

Nick punched the wall and regretted the action immediately as he must have hit a stud. Typing when his knuckles stung was difficult. **You are not a coward. Do you want help painting?**

The pendulum on the grandmother clock counted out the seconds as he waited for her answer. After last night, she was unlikely to let him come over.

—Have you ever painted before?

Once. Reverend Cavanagh had some unique ideas for making restitution for ones' crimes or accidents. The clock ticked louder.

—K

Do I need to bring anything? Paintbrush?

—Just wear old clothes if you have them.

I'll be over soon. Hopefully he could get there before she changed her mind.

Zoe picked up her phone to text Nick just as the bell buzzed. Too late to tell him not to come. Having him over to paint would be one of those things Candace would applaud her for. So would her therapist. Statistically, she knew not every man was like Mr. Dodd. Taking a deep breath, she opened the door.

"I brought bagels." He held up a bag and cup carrier. Even in a T-shirt and jeans, he managed to look slightly overdressed. Zoe opened the door wider and let him come in. "I also brought Lucinda's caramel cider."

Zoe took off her plastic gloves. "We should eat in the living room. The kitchen is out of commission."

"So, when did you start painting?" Nick set the food on the coffee table.

"Around four. I had to tape off the kitchen first. I didn't move the fridge out or the oven away from the wall. I figured I would get help with those."

"Nightmares?"

She skipped answering. "I was on the phone with Mom, then Candace, until after midnight."

"You're avoiding the question."

Zoe took a sip of the caramel cider. "Not much. You don't look well rested either."

"I didn't get much sleep. I don't like things I can't solve."

How could she explain that this wasn't something anyone could solve? It took time, friends, therapy, and prayer to reach a new level of normal. "You did a lot last night. Poor Sebastian. How long did he drive around?"

"Not as long as he would have if he thought you needed it, even if I weren't paying him." Nick took a bite of his bagel.

"Did you offer to fly me to Indiana to get me to react or because you meant it?"

"Both. If that's what you need, the offer stands. I couldn't let you out before I thought you would be all right. For me, that means an eye roll. If we are together for longer than an hour without one, I know I am not doing my job as a friend."

Zoe rolled her eyes just to make him smile. "You know I roll them on purpose now, don't you?"

He nodded. "It reminds me of something Sean's grandmother used to say about making faces and having it freeze like that."

"My grandma tells me if I am not careful, they will roll into the back of my head." So far today's normal was not too different than yesterday's. Nick still cared. Last time, her boyfriend had dumped her like a leftover fast-food meal that had been reheated too many times. He'd joined the others in spreading lies. Somehow her pain had become his embarrassment. And his false character witness was enough to get the district attorney to drop charges against her attacker, citing lack of evidence.

Finished with her cider, Zoe put a new pair of gloves on and handed a set to Nick. "Roller or brush?"

"What's the difference?"

"I thought you said you'd painted before."

"Once."

She tried not to roll her eyes. His smile told her she was unsuccessful. "I'll work on the edges with the brush, and you can work on the larger wall with the roller. The main thing is to make sure you don't have too much paint and to roll in *W* shapes." Zoe demonstrated.

"I can do that."

Zoe took the brush and worked on the area between the cupboard and the backsplash. After a few strokes, she checked Nick's progress. Paint dripped down the wall. "I think you need a bit less paint."

Nick put the roller back in the tray and started again.

"Roll it one more time over the ridge part. That's better." Zoe set her brush down and went to stand beside him. "Make the *W* bigger and wider."

Nicks next attempt wasn't much better.

Zoe moved closer and placed her hand over his. Electricity shot up her arm, and her heart raced the way it had last weekend when he'd held her hand during a movie. For a second, she forgot what she was doing. Nick didn't move until she guided his arm. "More like this." When they completed the reverse *W*, she let go and stepped back. For a second, he paused, then started painting. "That's better. Now, catch the drip near the door with your roller. If you smooth the drips out now, it will not show as much as if the paint starts to dry."

She returned to the space below the cupboards, her arm still feeling the contact, most of her body tingled. How was that possible? Last time she couldn't even look at her boyfriend or even hold hands. Almost every man she knew had become a villain waiting to strike. How could she have stood so close to Nick after last night? Her brain searched for answers. At least he didn't seem upset by it. *Don't overthink this, Zoe. It was a teaching moment. Nothing inappropriate.* She tried to concentrate on the wall in front of her. Nick hadn't seemed affected, so it shouldn't be a big deal. But it was.

Zoe moved to the area over the sink. Here, the old green resembled rotten pickle more than olive. Watching the walls change to a buttery yellow made her smile. If she had half the painting talent her roommates did, she might take on the cabinets with some fun designs. But this wasn't her kitchen.

A hand clamped down on her shoulder. She didn't think. She reacted.

"Ki-ah!"

The horror in Zoe's face matched the pain in Nick's. Zoe dropped her paintbrush and covered her mouth with her hand, and she started shaking. Nick lowered his hand from his eye. "Zoe. It's okay. See?"

She shook her head violently back and forth.

His eye stung.

"I'm sorry, I'm sorry, I'm sorry, I'm sorry." Her knees buckled, and she sunk to the floor.

Nick wished for wisdom. What would Sean's grandfather do? Pray. Did a simple "Help!" count? "Do you have any ice or frozen peas?"

Zoe crawled over to the icebox and used it to pull herself up. She pulled out a bag of blueberries. She winced as she handed them to him. "I'm so sorry."

"It's okay. I shouldn't have startled you. You didn't answer when I asked you a question." Nick walked to the couch and sat down. He would worry about the paint later. The sofa was Sean's old one. A few drops of yellow would improve it.

She followed him with a box of baby wipes. "I got paint all over your face." She handed him a wipe.

"Would you, please?"

She bit her lip. He shouldn't have pushed her to touch him. He opened his mouth to say so when she raised her hand to the cheek under his uninjured eye. Her touch was gentle, uncertain.

"Wipe as hard as you need. I am tougher than that." He kept his face as still as possible.

"I am so sorry." She wiped along his jawline.

Nick covered her hand with his. "I'm not angry. Where did you learn to fight? My bodyguards could take a lesson or two."

"I took self-defense and Tae-kwon-do classes last year."

Nick dropped his hand. "Why?"

"I wanted to be prepared." Zoe pulled out another wipe and cleaned the side of his nose.

"For what?"

"Last night."

Nick wondered if she would elaborate. She lifted the blueberry bag away from his eye. "They told me I needed to learn more control. I had too much anger. I didn't mean to hurt you." Her lip quivered, but her eyes remained dry.

"What were you thinking about when I was trying to get your attention?" He hoped he was asking the right questions.

Zoe took a deep breath. "I was trying not to think about last time and the trial."

"Last time?" The question came out before Nick could stop it.

She sat back and played with the wipe for a moment. She didn't look up. "I was raped."

He barely dared breathe. What should he say? Do? None of the awareness courses he'd reviewed for their businesses came to mind. *More help?*

Zoe didn't look up from the wipe she now folded into a neat square. "He was one of the teaching assistants. I didn't go to the hospital right away, so there wasn't much DNA evidence left. When I decided to press charges, he claimed the event was consensual. Told lies about me, even got someone to write in the campus paper about girls who cried wolf. The lies got to the point I could hardly walk across campus. After, my boyfriend falsely claimed I wasn't as innocent as I said I was. The DA dropped the case, citing lack of evidence. I got anonymous calls propositioning me. My grades plummeted, and I left school. Only my counselor, a few friends, and my family believed me. I am afraid if Mr. Dodd has a good attorney, they will find the records and news reports. And my life will be on repeat, everyone mocking and questioning. I don't know if I can face it a second time. And now I hit you, hurt you." She spoke the entire sentence in one breath, never looking up from the wipe she was playing with. A tear fell into her lap.

Instinctively, Nick understood that what he said next would determine everything in their relationship from that point on. He had learned from the classes that when someone experienced such a horrific ordeal, being able to talk about it freely was critical to their recovery. Everything he had read and every expert they'd consulted as they'd set up harassment policies advised they include counseling services for that reason. His next words could either make her feel as if she had been raped all over again or like she had someone she could add to her circle of trusted friends. "Thank you for trusting me enough to tell me."

He held out his free hand, palm up, hoping she would take it. Needing her to trust him. It wouldn't change anything between them. A Lie. Her trust would change everything. He wanted to crush the TA and smack the boyfriend, hunt down the prank callers, and erase her memory. He couldn't do those things. Instead, he waited.

She dropped the wipe in her lap, her hand hovering over his for a moment before she laid it on his. Although she didn't raise her eyes above the center of his shirt, relief filled him. "Everyone will find out soon enough. Social media posts named me the "cry wolf girl." The newspapers never did, but it didn't matter since they printed the opinion pieces. The connection isn't hard to make."

He wanted to pull her into a hug and keep her there until all her pain melted away, but a certain stiffness in her prevented his doing so. "This won't be like last time. There are videos of Dodd chasing after you. Security witnessed what he was yelling. There is evidence. Your employer believed you, and I believe you." Nick

102

would have continued, but she would not have appreciated his thoughts because they involved his money. There were many legal means for money to save a reputation, and he would use them all if necessary.

Zoe looked at him, wide-eyed. "You do?"

He rubbed his thumb along the back of her hand. "From day one you have been nothing but honest with me. Do you know how many people would tell me they didn't like me to my face? I believe you." It may be that those three words had more power in them than any other three words he could say.

She wiped away the tears with her fingertips, smudging a dab of paint across her cheek. "I didn't exactly say I didn't like you." The corner of her mouth raised as if she were trying to smile.

"Close enough. How badly do you want to finish painting the kitchen?" That was one disaster his money could fix.

She stared at the half-painted kitchen space before answering. "Not so much at the moment."

"Let's go out to Blue Pines. You can visit with Tessa, and I can go hide away in my man cave with a steak on my eye."

"I need to clean up." Letting go of his hand, she stood.

"Can I help?"

Zoe reddened. "I meant me, not the kitchen. I need to clean up in there, too."

Nick felt his face heat. "Do you want me to leave?"

"You need to keep those berries on your eye. I trust you'll sit here until I am done." Zoe went into the kitchen.

She trusted him enough to let him stay while she showered. Even before she told him she trusted him, she'd allowed him in her apartment without a third party. He sat a moment, letting that fact sink in. She trusted him.

Nick adjusted his makeshift ice pack and pulled out his phone so he could text Sean. **Zoe needs to visit Tessa ASAP. Can you two meet us at the Cottage?**

—We are at the church. Can you come to the old house?

Yes, clear as much of Tessa's day as possible.
—Why?
Will tell you when we get there.

Zoe finished in the kitchen and went down the hall. Nick heard a door shut and a lock click. A moment later, the pipes creaked, a sure sign she had seen the paint in her hair. Time to make a couple of calls while she couldn't hear him.

Finding Colin's number in his contacts, Nick pressed dial.

"Do you have a minute? I need help with a problem."

"You've got them too?" Colin sounded as exhausted as Nick felt.

"Not exactly me. Zoe. I need you to erase everything you can legally; find any place on the web, especially social media, for the last two or three years."

"That is a tall and vague order."

"You are the only person I know who can do it."

"Do I get to know why?" The click of computer keys echoed in the background.

He didn't feel comfortable telling Zoe's story. "I think you will figure it out soon enough. Can I help you with your problems?"

"Unless you understand women, probably not. I goofed, and Candace isn't talking to me. I think she left town with Mandy. I took the wrong door out of the friend zone."

"Hey, I finally found my way into the friend zone. Might I suggest you let her give you a black eye?" Nick lifted the berries and checked his vision. It wasn't blurry. Still, he couldn't open it fully.

"There is a story there. Maybe we can get things to change by the premiere."

"Premiere?" What had he missed? Zoe hadn't mentioned anything.

"The Hearthfire Christmas movie Sean and Tessa were scenery for. Mandy and Candace have been working on plans for weeks now in the old theater in Blue Pines."

"I don't think I got an invite."

"Oh, you will. They haven't sent them yet. I'll just—" Colin paused. The clicking of his keyboard intensified. "Oya, that is why

Zoe transferred schools her senior year. This guy smeared her in everything from the university paper to the most unpopular social media websites. Why do people have to be such jerks?"

"I wish I knew." The pipes creaked again. He only had a few more minutes.

"Give me a couple hours. I can't do much about the newspapers other than trying to boost other things in the rankings in front of them. The papers don't say her name, but with the social media posts, I managed to connect them quickly. If there are court records, I can't touch those. However, she still shouldn't be named. Did you know Zoe won a few awards for her design, including one for Wolf Trap, the National Park, and at the county fair for 4-H things? I'll push those stories to the top in the searches. Anyone specific I need to hide this from?"

Nick adjusted the berry pack. Most of the fruit was soft now. "Sleazy lawyers ..."

"I'll do my best. With any luck, they will only find her detasseling-corn speed record and her prize heifer during a preliminary search and won't look further. A bullying complaint to a couple of the networks should delete some of this permanently. They are too afraid of lawsuits. See you at the premiere."

Nick dialed Sebastian. Given the slit he was seeing out of in his left eye, he probably shouldn't drive in Manhattan traffic. He requested a backup driver come and move his personal car from the parking space back to the garage.

Zoe emerged. His sisters were never that fast. Her hair was still damp and up in a messy bun, her face devoid of makeup.

"Sorry I took so long. I had paint in my hair." Clearly she didn't know the meaning of a long shower.

Nick handed her the berries and stood. "I think those are useless now. Sebastian will be here in five. Do you mind if I go look in your mirror?"

Nodding, Zoe grimaced before taking the defrosted berries into the kitchen.

The mirror didn't lie. Good thing he already had the shades-and-baseball-cap thing down. If he stayed out of the public eye for a few days, he might be able to avoid any questions.

sixteen

ZOE TRIED NOT TO APOLOGIZE the entire ride out to Blue Pines. What would she tell Sean and Tessa? And Nick's parents? She looked out the window so she wouldn't have to see Nick holding the ice pack Sebastian had brought him.

Nick took her hand in his freezing one on the seat between them. She glanced at him to see he had removed the ice pack. He smiled a slightly crooked smile. "I think I have had the ice on long enough for this round. Even my teeth are starting to freeze."

Nodding was all she could muster for a response. If she started talking, she wasn't sure what would come out. She didn't want to pour out her heart with Sebastian listening.

Sebastian pulled into the driveway of Sean's grandfather's old house. "Shall I wait here?"

Nick leaned forward and dropped the reusable ice pack over the seat. "Let me talk with Sean, then I'll know my plans."

Sebastian opened Zoe's door. Nick followed her out without letting go of her hand.

Sean opened the front door. He started to say something, but Nick shook his head and put up a hand.

"Tessa will be here in a moment. She had to pick something up on her way back from the studio. Can I get you anything?"

Nick led Zoe to the old couch. "I'm fine. Zoe?"

"Water, please?"

Sean disappeared into the kitchen and returned with a glass of water, which he handed to Zoe before sitting down in one of the chairs. "May I ask now?"

Zoe opened her mouth, but Nick spoke first. "It was an accident. I stood in the right place at the wrong time."

"I punched him." Zoe hung her head to avoid Sean's reaction.

"Good for you! I've been trying to get a swing in for over twenty-five years." Sean's voice held a bit of the levity that had been missing from the morning.

Zoe raised her head. "I didn't want to hit him."

"Perhaps you don't know him well enough, then." Sean smiled.

Nick returned Sean's grin. "Sean, not everyone remembers me sticking worms in their mud pies."

Tessa opened the front door before the conversation got any more awkward. Zoe's eyes widened at the sight of her blue-haired cousin. "Candace, what are you doing here?"

Zoe ran across the room and hugged Candace.

"I heard Sean and Tessa were having a party, and thought I would drop by."

Tessa looked at the men. "Sebastian is still in the driveway. We need girl time. Since there is chocolate in the house and none at the new one, we claim this as our temporary girls' clubhouse."

Surprise filled both Tessa's and Candace's faces when Nick stood and turned toward them. But to Zoe's relief, neither of them asked any questions.

"I'll take Nick over to see the new carpet. We'll have Sebastian drive us." Sean kissed his wife before leaving.

Nick stopped in front of Zoe. "Enjoy today and stop worrying about my eye."

As soon as the door shut, Zoe turned to Candace. "What are you doing here?"

"Last night when I got your 911 text, I was on the phone with Mandy, which is why I didn't pick up your call but called you back when I got the text. After you hung up, I called Mandy back and told them I thought we should all get together now. Abbie got involved, and around six this morning, we headed for the airport. Mandy and Abbie are down at the theater with baby Joy. Your being here saved us coming into town to surprise you. Now, what happened to Nick's eye?"

The women sat on the old couches, and Zoe recounted the events of the morning as well as a condensed version of the night before for Tessa's benefit.

"How did Nick react?" asked Tessa.

"Stunned but not angry. I know his eye has got to hurt, but he is too nice to complain about it. I'm not sure what to do." Zoe wrung her hands. "He says he believes me about everything." The thought still filled her with awe.

Candace grabbed Zoe's hands in her own. "Question time with Candace. What is most upsetting to you, your boss or Nick's eye?"

"Nick's eye."

"Why?"

"Because I should have been in control. I hurt him." She'd put all her force behind that punch.

Tessa moved to Zoe's other side on the couch. "I have a question. Think back to yesterday at this time. Where did you think your relationship with Nick was headed?"

Without checking her reflection in the mirror above the mantel, Zoe knew she was blushing. "Toward a kiss. I realized he was one of the good guys Candace and my therapist point out are the majority of people. I trust him more now. Can you believe I took a shower knowing he was in the apartment and we had no third party?"

Candace nodded her acknowledgment. "Easier than you can. Where are you headed now?"

"I don't know. I only blurted out my deepest, darkest secret to him, and he didn't react like I expected. I've been waiting for him to run away from me all morning. At least he didn't react like some of the guys did back—" Zoe couldn't finish the sentence.

"He still treated you with respect?"

Zoe nodded her answer to her cousin's question.

"Next question: Now that he knows about your past, do you still want to move your relationship past friends?" Candace held Zoe's gaze with hers.

Zoe took a deep breath. "I wish I could, but partially to erase the feel of Mr. Dodds' crushing me. I want to relax and enjoy a kiss. I need to, so I know I can. But I don't want to turn a kiss into a science experiment."

Tessa asked the next question. "Do you think you can be this honest with him?"

Zoe stared into the fireplace. Could she talk to Nick or any guy like this? "I don't know."

Tessa drew her into a hug. "I think when you know you can discuss your greatest fears with a man, he is the one you keep forever."

Candace shifted next to her. Zoe wondered if Tessa was talking to more than just her in this conversation. Pulling back from the hug, she turned to Candace. "Candace you never said why you were on the phone with Tessa and Mandy in the first place. What is going on?"

"I told Colin about *all* of my cancer in a moment of temper, and now I can't face him."

"Now it's time for "Questions with Zoe. So, what happened?"

Sean concluded the house tour. "Are you going to tell me more about your black eye? Or am I going to get more convenient excuses like I am from Tessa about half the roommates descending this weekend?"

"I am not sure how much of the story is mine to tell. Some of Zoe's story you need to know anyway. Who knows what will happen if someone hears the 911 call."

"You called 911 over a black eye?" Sean went into the kitchen, Nick following.

"No, I called 911 because Zoe was locked in a closet hiding from her boss, who assaulted her." At Sean's shocked expression, Nick amended his statement. "Not Adrian. The art director—or former art director. Adrian fired him on the spot. Zoe texted me, and fortunately, building security got to her before her boss could. She left him looking worse than I do. But she wasn't entirely unscathed. Most likely he will be charged with aggravated assault of some degree. I want to keep it out of the papers, but if some reporter—" There was no point in finishing the thought. Sean was learning just how nosy some so-called reporters could be. Nick sat down on one of the kitchen stools. "This morning I tapped Zoe on the shoulder. Her mind was in another place. I should have known better."

"You have paint in your hair and on your shirt—the same color Tessa chose for the apartment kitchen. Was she painting?" Sean tossed Nick an apple and a water bottle.

"We were painting. I will have you know I am becoming adept at the use of a roller. That reminds me. You probably should get a crew over there to finish the job before all the drips become permanent." Nick bit into his apple.

"What I should do is buy the building and restore it to a single-family home."

"Yes, you should."

Sean stared at his old friend. "I thought you were against it."

"I was against you making rash decisions with your newfound wealth. The price dropped by $6 mil this week, bringing the brownstone back into a more reasonable price range. You have also not given up the idea in ten months. I say buy. Your biggest obstacle will be Mrs. Clark. She has lived there since the day she was born in 1945, but since she used to babysit you, I am sure you can talk her into moving with a nice enticement. The rent on her place is one of the lowest in the city." Nick tossed the apple core in the trash.

"How did you know the price dropped?" Sean folded his arms and leaned against the counter.

"I wouldn't have let the place get away from you. Now, can I head over to the Cottage? I would like to get cleaned up before we see the women again." He also wanted to be the one to explain to his parents. He didn't often attract media attention, but this situation could blow up quickly, even if Dodd took a plea deal. Hopefully Dad could help him stay one step ahead.

By the time Mandy and Abbie joined them, there were few secrets to share. Zoe shared the briefest of outlines with the other women. Abbie complimented Zoe on her choice of moves and reassured her most black eyes looked worse than they were. "I've given all of my brothers black eyes at one time or another. Alan's received three. He tucks his chin and forgets I'm shorter." Only Abbie could pass off a black eye as an everyday occurrence. Zoe had met the four Hastings brothers on several occasions and had to agree there was no lasting damage.

"I still can't believe you came out here for me." Zoe helped herself to a piece of the cheesecake Mandy had bought on her way from the theater to the house. If only she'd had this kind of support last time. It had been her mother and Candace who'd talked her into having the belated rape-kit test and reporting the assault to campus officials. But only her mother had been able to drop everything and drive to be at her side.

"I came for the cheesecake. I've been craving real New York cheesecake all week. So much better than craving pickles." Abbie took a large bite. There still was no sign of a baby bump, but Abbie still exercised like a bodyguard, minus the sparring with her brothers.

Tessa held up her hands. "Don't you look at me, I'm not the one in the family way. You'll know I am when I start staying out of the glass shop and do all my designing on the computer." The thought hadn't crossed Zoe's mind, but from the look Mandy wore on her face, someone had had time to think about babies.

Mandy bounced Joy on her hip. "I didn't hear anyone ask. Speaking of which—has anyone heard from Araceli?"

"Not this week. They were going down to Haiti with a fall group of homeschooling families. Connections can be so spotty, so I don't think she even tries to text or email us anymore when she is there." Tessa sat down at the old Formica-topped kitchen table. "Did you finish everything you need to at the theater?"

Mandy nodded. "Yes, the world premiere of Hearthfire's Christmas movie will be shown on November 2, with bonus showings the next day. Anyone with a Blue Pines address can get into the Saturday showings free. Friday night is invitation only, focusing on the locals who were also extras or had their businesses used as sets."

"I'm still torn about if I want our first kiss to be in there or not." Tessa blushed. Zoe couldn't blame her. Having a first kiss, even a staged one, shown to all the world was not on her bucket list.

"I wonder how long it will be until someone figures out Hearthfire paid America's newest billionaire fifty dollars to kiss the woman he married. I defy their writers to come up with a better story. Every news show in the country is going to want you for their feel-good Christmas spotlight." Heads nodded at Candace's observation.

Tessa took her empty plate to the sink. "I can't believe no one at Hearthfire has figured out we are in the background. That's what makes me think our kiss isn't in there. I don't look forward to the media buzz."

Abbie made a face. "I never watched those morning shows before I was engaged, and after making a couple rounds of the shows with our fake-engagement-to-real-wedding thing, I refuse to watch them on principle. I tried to extract a promise from

Preston that we would never have to do an interview again. He told me I should have put it in a prenup."

Zoe laughed. "Like you had time in the three hours you were engaged to think of such a thing."

"Knock, knock. Is it safe for us guys to join you?" Sean stood in the half-open doorway.

"Come on in. You can finish the cheesecake." Tessa kissed her husband before handing him a plate.

Candace stage-whispered, "Who needs to watch the Hearthfire movie when we have the real thing right here?"

Tessa winked. "And it all started with a kiss."

Zoe looked at Nick and couldn't help but wonder if their story had started with a fist. Not the story she wanted to tell in years to come, but something had started.

seventeen

Nick rolled up the window between the back seat and Sebastian.

Zoe shot him a look.

Nick didn't care. Now was as good a time as any to talk. Help was only forty-two inches away if she felt uncomfortable.

"I would like to talk, and this seemed like the best place. Privacy and a witness if you need it to feel comfortable." It had been his mother's suggestion.

"Like an old-fashioned chaperone?"

"Who at this moment is conveniently deaf and probably won't blink an eye if one of us moves to the middle seat so I can finally hug you like I have wanted to since this morning."

Zoe turned in her seat to face him better. "Why *didn't* you hug me this morning?"

"I was torn. But I felt I should let you take the step if you wanted to, not because you felt you had to."

"And now?"

"It's still your choice." He opened his arms, hoping she would choose to move to the center seat.

Zoe ran her thumb along the edge of the cross-body portion of her seat belt. "You know, if I accept your hug, I might cry some more."

"I'm fine with that." He would even take a punch in the other eye if it helped her come to terms with things and allowed her to move forward.

Zoe released the latch on her seat belt. Nick waited for her to slide across the seat to him, then circled his arms around her and held her as the tears started. Soon he felt her relax. She produced a tissue from a pocket and leaned into his side, dabbing at her tears.

"We should get the center belt on you before Sebastian yells at us over the intercom."

Zoe reached for the belt. "He can do that?"

Nick helped her get the end into the latch. "Can and will." He rested his arm around her shoulder as he brought her into a side embrace.

"I've needed this hug all day, but I didn't dare ask."

Nick wished he had offered sooner, but he had no idea how to balance what she needed with his own feelings. Next time Nick saw Sean, he owed him for the excellent advice. "Anytime you need a hug, you have an open invitation. No need to ask."

She nodded against his shoulder. "Are you okay with what I told you this morning?"

"You mean do-I-want-to-find-the-TA-and-make-the-next-ten-years-of-his-life-miserable-for-what-he-did-to-you okay, or I-still-want-you-in-my-life-because-you-make-me-smile-and-laugh-more-than-anyone-I-know okay?"

Zoe pulled back so she could study his face. "You really don't think less of me, do you?"

"Why would I?" It was a question he hadn't anticipated.

Zoe settled back into his embrace. Nick waited for Zoe to answer as he watched the lights of the city skyline take shape.

"I don't know, but some people do. They assume I was drunk, or did something to put myself in a vulnerable position, or that I am lying to justify having—"

He felt more than heard the tears start again. He kissed the top of her head, hoping the gesture showed his acceptance. "Then those people don't know you."

Zoe relaxed. She produced another tissue and wiped her eyes.

Nick watched buildings and signs pass, debating about the next questions he needed to ask. Was there any way they wouldn't be awkward?

Nick's heartbeat pulsed below her ear. She'd once read the safest sound in the world was a strong heartbeat—an instinct going back to what a baby heard in its mother's womb. Zoe agreed with the article.

Suddenly his heart rate sped up. "I need to ask you something else. When I envisioned what we could do this weekend, I hoped our time together would end in a kiss. But given what happened last night, I don't know what you feel. And I don't want things to feel as awkward as this question or worse."

Funny, she had thought a racing heart was more figurative than literal. Hers sped up too. "Are you asking permission?"

His heart still raced. "Not for this second, but later, if the moment is right, how will I know you are in the same place I am?"

"You mean other than the eye-to-eye-to-mouth triangle you have already done?" At least five times. Enough to have her pondering a kiss.

"What triangle?"

Zoe sat up a bit. "It is in all the movies and even some of the better cartoons. He looks into one eye, then the other, then down to her mouth, then back to the first eye. She mimics him or gives a hint of a smile. The camera pans in, and a swoon-worthy kiss follows." She was aware she was doing it as she explained and hoped he couldn't tell in the dim lighting.

"You say I've done this?"

"Have you thought about kissing me?"

Nick cleared his throat. "Possibly."

Zoe settled back into his side. Looking at his face made the conversation more embarrassing. "Then you have done the triangle. Candace says the pattern is a natural human response."

"Oh, so if I do the triangle thing and you smile, I can kiss you?"

"I won't even give you a black eye. But not tonight, please. My emotions have been on overdrive all day, and right after this conversation, a kiss would be awkward."

"Agreed. So, how about those Giants?"

Zoe smiled. "That was a subtle change of topic. I thought you were a Jets fan."

Nick laughed. "Sorry, the game was on TV, and it was the first thing I could think of."

Zoe took a deep breath. "Back to the other topic for a second. I need you to know I was thinking about kissing you yesterday morning too. I really don't know how my body or emotions might react, so if the time seems right and I push back or something, please, just–" Filled with embarrassment, she buried her face into his side.

His arm tightened around her, and after a moment, his other hand lifted her chin. "We will figure this out, and I'll try to keep an open mind as long as you can keep an open heart."

Zoe nodded and settled back into his arms for the rest of the ride, the smell of cinnamon and sandalwood surrounding her in her new safe place, her fears about the future slipping away.

Nick watched all the familiar buildings out the window, wishing Sebastian would drive them around the city again. Instead, he found a parking space a block away from the brownstone. "May I walk you up?"

Zoe nodded and sat up.

He put his arm back around her shoulders as they walked. "There is something you should know. I asked Colin to do everything he legally could to bury any part of the last couple years of your life on the web. I should have asked your permission, but I was more than a little angry." After talking with his mother, he realized he had overstepped, even if it was with good intentions.

"I thought of asking Colin last year, but I didn't want him to know, and I didn't know him well enough to admit I needed help."

"Sean also sent painters to clean up our mess. Do you mind if I wait while you check your apartment?" Nick didn't want to give her a choice.

"Do you mean do I mind if you are a bit hyperprotective? No." Zoe unlocked the front door.

Nick walked her upstairs. Other than the smell of paint, everything seemed to be in order. "Good night, Zoe. Do you want a ride back to Blue Pines tomorrow?"

"No, they are coming into the city to shop. Daniel and Preston are supposed to be here in the morning. I am not sure what they are doing. Night, Nick." Zoe rose up on her toes.

Nick froze.

She brushed a kiss on the cheek under his good eye.

Before he could blink, she was gone. The dead bolt slid shut. He imagined her looking through the peephole and smiled. "Sweet dreams, Zoe."

Nick jogged back down the stairs. Unlike Colin, he had found the right door out of the friend zone.

At the bottom of the stairs, he texted Sean to see if there were any plans for Saturday he could join.

—Dinner at the new house, 7 p.m. Be here at 6.

Done.

—Tessa says no more texting.

Oops. Sorry, Tessa.

When he got back in the car, he found the dividing window lowered. "My wife prepared her super-secret poultice. She swears the herbs and essential oils will decrease healing time by half. She wants us to pick it up before I drop you off. Does that suit you?"

"How bad does this one stink?"

"About the same as the rest of them."

Nick had been subject to several of Sebastian's wife's cures over the years. They all worked, but they all smelled like a roadkill skunk.

"Then it will work. Let's go." The smell would be worth getting the dark-purple bruise to disappear, if only so Zoe could stop wincing.

eighteen

NICK'S MONDAY MORNING TEXT CAME only seconds after her alarm went off.

—I'm a text away if you need me today. "You are braver than you believe, stronger than you seem, and smarter than you think." —Christopher Robin

You know that quote is only in the movie, not the book, right?

—Yes, but it still fits.

I'll need it today. A soak in the old-fashioned claw-foot tub with a lavender bath bomb and a drop of cinnamon oil on her pillow had kept the old nightmares away, but she still did not sleep soundly. Her mind kept running through what-ifs. The pillow hadn't quite smelled enough like Nick to relax her.

—Sebastian wants to drive you to work.

Tell him thanks, but I will take the subway. I need to start today off normally.

—Dinner with me tonight?

Pick me up from work?

—What about normal?

I don't know that I need to end my day with my usual ride home. If things went poorly at work, she didn't want to be on the subway.

—5:30?

Yes. I'll text you if that changes.

Zoe took extra care dressing for work. All four of her friends had bought her new blouses, none of them even remotely resembling the one that was destroyed. She wore the one Candace chose. Today she needed all the strength she could channel from her cousin, who, after years of dealing with cancer, was the strongest person she knew.

On the subway, Zoe couldn't bring herself to read the news. She settled on an ebook instead.

James got on at his stop and found a spot next to her.

Zoe took a breath. *So it begins.*

"How are you doing?" James swayed near her with the movement of the train.

"I had a good weekend. And you?"

"I'm not sure yet. Gina will be back from LA today. If Adrian and Shayne make her the new art director, I'll be as happy as a kid with a new puppy."

Zoe studied his face. "That is pretty happy."

"I think almost everyone is happy."

"Almost?"

"April is having a tough time. Dodd mentored her. He did a lot of things to make her work environment accessible beyond ADA requirements. But then, you are her friend."

Zoe nodded. Above them, the voice announced their stop. She followed James out of the subway. He stopped at the corner coffee shop. Zoe decided to wait for him rather than continue on her own. James handed her a cup. "And I don't even have a job for you today."

"So this is just because?"

"Because today will be hard and you need a good start."

Zoe took a sip. "Thanks."

She went through the first five minutes of her Monday as normally as possible. April didn't say hello, and the floor seemed quieter than normal. She checked her tablet. No one seemed to need her, so she pulled up one of her projects and started to work. The tablet pinged.

Accept 9:30 meeting with Adrian Scott? Location: his office.

She clicked the Accept button. There wasn't much of a choice. In the ten minutes she'd worked, she'd changed the font twice and the size of a photo once. She went up to the top floor and presented herself to Adrian's office assistant.

"Go on in, Miss Wilson. They are ready."

They? She opened the door to find Adrian Scott, Shayne Ricks, and Maurene, the PR woman from the 9/11 museum dedication. There was another man she didn't recognize.

Adrian stood. "Have a seat, Zoe. This isn't as imposing as it looks. You know Shayne. And I believe you met Maurene from PR. This is Stirling, head of Human Resources."

Zoe sat in the chair Adrian indicated.

He sat as well. "We have been looking at our policies over the weekend. We also contacted all of the female employees who left our employ suddenly in the last few years."

"Two of them have also said they were assaulted by Mr. Dodd but were too afraid to come forward. Your bravery gave them the courage," said Shayne. "What we don't understand is why no one reported or complained. There was the one report six months ago by an employee for inappropriate comments. Mr. Dodd was reprimanded and sent to a sensitivity training. How did we miss this?" She turned to Zoe.

"In hindsight, is there anything we could have done to prevent this?" asked Stirling.

Zoe thought back. "I knew Mr. Dodd wasn't popular with some of the employees. April said something bad happens to people who work late. She wasn't specific, and given her reaction to what I told her, I don't think she knew. She had just observed a pattern. Since so few employees talk to her socially, she relies on observation."

Maurene tapped her pen. "Did April say anything definitive?"

"Not really. Just that she liked me and hoped I wouldn't stay late because she had two other friends who stayed late and then quit unexpectedly." Zoe gave a little shrug.

"I knew Dodd wasn't admired by some of the employees. I don't understand how we could have so colossally failed to see this side of him." Stirling shook his head.

"Do you have any ideas about what we can do to prevent this, moving forward?" asked Maurene.

"What is your current method of reporting harassment? It occurred to me that I don't know. The policy isn't exactly the type of thing I'd want to be caught looking up on my tablet."

"They come to file a complaint in the office or by email," said Stirling.

"Is there a way to turn in an anonymous tip or report?" asked Zoe.

"No."

"I would set up a way to call or email anonymously, then put the contact information in the bathrooms."

Adrian leaned forward. "Why the bathrooms?"

"If someone is harassed and they want to be alone, they will go to the bathroom. And bathrooms are boring places, so the information would get read if there wasn't an emergency."

"We could put a complaint box in the restrooms for nonviolent harassment. It could help," said Maurene.

Adrian checked the clock. "It is almost time for your Monday morning meeting. Shayne and I are going down too. We just need to wrap up some other items."

"I don't know if it helps, but you could not have prevented what happened. I do appreciate your quick actions." Zoe left the room.

She entered the elevator alone, glad for a few moments of quiet time. *They believed me.* Not once had they accused her of anything or insinuated it was her fault.

They believed me!! She would have done a victory dance, but the cameras were watching.

Monday morning, Nick opted to work from home. The skunk cure was working, just not fast enough. Spending most of the weekend in Blue Pines, he'd avoided any questions. He wondered all morning how Zoe's day was going. When his phone pinged a text at lunchtime, he couldn't get to it fast enough.

—A good day so far. Gina is the new art director. S&R are making changes to their harassment-policy procedures. Most people are treating me the same.

The word *most* triggered a flag. **But?**

—April won't talk to me. James is trying to make up for it. Overall, it is a good day.

Still on for tonight?

—5:30. I'll be waiting.

See you then.

Now Nick needed to figure out what to do tonight. He had all the money in the world and the Big Apple at his feet and not a single idea for a date. He called Sean. His friend knew the lower, critical parts of the city better than he did. He wanted to stay under the radar and avoid anyone with a camera. It would be easier to have dinner and a movie at his place, but he didn't think she was ready for that step.

An hour and three phone calls later, Nick had the perfect date planned. He checked his weather app—well, perfect unless Mother Nature decided to crash the party.

Now to wait for five thirty. He looked at his papers and laughed. Nick had gotten his wish. He was just as useless as Sean had been this summer.

Gina called Zoe into her office. When she entered, Gina asked her to shut the door. "How are you doing?"

Zoe wasn't sure how to answer. Better than she thought she would be, but not as good as she hoped.

"Too broad of a question. I know I can't answer that question today either. I have the job I have wanted for years but at a terrible cost. I supervised all the women he—" Gina took several deep breaths. "I never saw it. I knew he wasn't the nicest person but—. That isn't why I called you in. It seems when the game of musical chairs is done, there will be a vacancy for a new junior designer. I'd like you to consider taking the position."

Zoe blinked. "Me? I haven't graduated yet."

"But you will when this internship is over. Take a few days to think about it. We still need to fill my old position. Adrian has said they will redecorate and rearrange the offices on this side of the floor. I don't want Wayne's office, and I don't think anyone else does either. Adrian had security clean it out and deliver his personal effects to his home. I can't imagine what his wife is going through. How many lives can one person destroy?"

Zoe didn't have an answer for that.

"I know April is having a hard time with this. She'll come around eventually. Give her some space. I'm not going to assign you to work with her for a week. Are you all right working with James? I know from experience that working closely with a man after an assault can be hard."

"You too?"

"Yup, me too. It wasn't here, and it wasn't Wayne. I thought I would recognize the signs. I can't believe I didn't." Gina shook her head.

"You know, HR was looking for ideas. I wonder if a support group would be helpful. We wouldn't feel so alone."

"I'll suggest it." Gina typed a note into her tablet.

"As for working with James, I am fine with it." Zoe didn't mention that she was quite sure he wasn't interested in any of the females in the office. It wasn't her business.

"To be honest, half the men in the department are a bit scared of you after they saw what you did to Mr. Dodd. Someone found his mugshot online and passed it around Friday." Gina gave her a satisfied smile.

"I don't want to see it."

"I don't blame you. I have taken self-defense classes, but I don't think I could use it. I think I would be too afraid."

"I thought so too. I froze, then the adrenalin kicked in. If you ever have to use those skills, you can." If it weren't for Nick's eye, she would be pleased with herself. She had taken down an assailant and gotten away.

Gina's desk phone rang, and she reached for it, holding up a finger for Zoe to wait. The conversation was brief and monosyllabic. Gina hung up. "Well, that was interesting. They are going to start the remodel tomorrow. I'd better call a quick meeting so we can get these offices cleaned out. Adrian is on his way down."

For the second time in a day, Adrian joined them for a department meeting. "When we asked for permission to do some light construction, I expected the approval to take weeks, not hours. Even the permits have been fast-tracked. This is going to make for a bit of togetherness. Some time ago, Gina suggested that instead of individual cubicles, we move to pods of four employees serving as teams. The design she created and modified by the architect saves floor space and creates a more open working environment. Each pod will have a lead designer and will be based on current work teams. There will be a crew coming at 5:00 p.m. to start rearranging. I have ordered banker's boxes, which will be here as soon as possible, to pack up your things. I have asked for volunteers from other departments to come to help empty the old art director's office and help anyone who needs it. Label your equipment, including chairs and computers. Remove everything from your drawers and shelves. Label extra shelves if you had them." He turned to Gina. "Is there any critical project that losing the rest of the afternoon of work will jeopardize?"

Gina asked a couple of the designers. "I think we will be fine."

"Those of you who currently have offices on the south wall, we need to find space for you. Project managers, there are three empty cubicles up in Public Relations. I know it isn't as convenient as being down here, but you can be moved tonight. Gina, there is an empty—"

Gina raised a hand to interrupt Adrian. "I think a temporary private cubicle where the layout shows a smaller meeting area will work best for me."

The elevators opened, a courier with a hand truck exited.

"And there are your boxes. Have fun." Adrian left.

Gina waved her arm as if casting a spell. "Let the chaos begin."

Zoe joined the others in moving and packing. As the intern, she had less stuff than anyone else.

She stepped on April's doorbell. "Need help?"

April set down the cup of pens she held. "Why would you help me?"

"Why not?"

"I called you a liar."

"I understand. It doesn't matter." Zoe kept the conversation in sign. "I've been called worse."

"We are still friends?"

"Sure. Now, do you need help?"

April smiled. "I have collected too many books."

"I'll go find another box."

Today was turning out to be better than she ever thought it could. And it was going to end with a date with Nick.

Nick hung up the phone. Somehow he'd convinced two competing contractors to work together to speed up the remodel on the building where Scott & Ricks was located. An architect had been emailing plans back and forth with the design firm for the past couple hours. The initial drafts had been signed off on, and final drafts were being drawn. Nick hadn't balked at the rush fee his favorite architectural firm requested. He was still kicking himself for not realizing how a small remodel would help the employees to move on and any other women who might have been Dodd's victims start to heal.

It had been Adrian's idea after the employee he'd promoted refused to move into the vacated office. Nick only wished they had thought of it on Friday.

His phone pinged. Zoe.

—**I'll be finished at 4:30. Office remodel underway.**

Not quite done here. I'll send Sebastian.

—**No need. I'll go change. Pick me up at the apartment.**

Don't change too much. I like you the way you are.

—**Ha, ha. BTW, I can't help but wonder what the building owner paid to get the construction fast-tracked.**

Nothing.

—**Or will pay.**

He sent a winky-face emoji.

—**That is what I thought. Thanks.**

It was the first time she'd accepted him spending money on her without a fight. Of course, she had no idea how much money he was adding to the budget Adrian had outlined. With any luck, she would never know.

nineteen

"IT WASN'T SUPPOSED TO RAIN tonight. Only a 20 percent chance." Nick smiled apologetically as he helped Zoe back into the car.

"It was bound to happen. You planned a picnic in a roof garden in October. That was too tempting for Murphy to pass up."

"Murphy?" Nick played with his cuff links again. Today he wore a set engraved with a G.

"As in Murphy's law. Did you know you play with your cuff links when you don't have an answer?"

"You noticed?"

"Of course. I like the horse ones you wore last week."

He straightened the links. "Now I am at a loss as to what to do."

When Zoe pondered suggesting his penthouse, her mother's voice echoed in her head, warning her that it might not be the best idea. Not because Nick would take advantage of her, but because she might take advantage of him.

"Might I suggest the atrium?" Sebastian changed lanes.

Nick smiled. "Best idea of the night. Let me make a call."

Zoe followed the paths of the raindrops down the window and half listened to the call, not caring where Nick chose. Dinner at Lucinda's would be fine. Nick wanted a picnic. She supposed anything was possible in New York.

When Sebastian pulled into the underground garage of Gooding Tower, Zoe's curiosity was piqued. Where could one have a picnic in an office building? They parked in a reserved space. Only a handful of cars remained as most employees had left for the day.

Nick gathered the salvaged picnic dinner from the trunk. Zoe reached for the blanket but thought better of it. It was too damp. Sebastian opened a duffel and pulled out two blankets in vacuum bags. "Take these. Even an indoor picnic needs a blanket."

Nick used a keypad to access the elevators. He chose the fiftieth floor, and the elevator sped upward. Zoe's stomach wasn't prepared for the speed. Or maybe it was the way Nick held her hand that sent the butterflies fighting against gravity.

Rain beat on the glass roof of the atrium. In the distance, lightning flashed. Lights dotted the East River. On a clear day, the view must be spectacular. She needed to come back. "I love the sound of rain. And all the benefits of staying dry." Zoe spun in a circle, trying to take in all the plants, flowers, and trees growing in the enclosed space.

Nick laughed and caught her around the waist. Her spin stopped with her hand on his chest. His heart was racing as fast as hers. His other hand cupped her face. She couldn't help smiling as his eyes traveled the triangle. She went up on her toes so her lips met his. The sound of the rain faded, and old memories died. The faint taste of cinnamon marked the kiss as his. There was only this kiss erasing the past, giving life to the present, and promising a future.

Nick ended the kiss and pulled back enough to rest his forehead on hers. "I was going wait to do that until after dessert."

"Don't you know it's best to start on dessert first?" Zoe used his tie to tug him into another kiss. A place in her heart healed, and her mind stilled. For two years she'd worried she would never want to kiss a man again. Now she wondered if she ever wanted to stop.

Thunder clapped, and the windows shook.

Zoe jerked back, her eyes darting along the glass-and-metal roof. "Is it safe to be in here?"

The moment was gone. Nick found her hands and led her to the blanket he'd spread out when she started twirling. He helped her sit and then sat beside her. "It is very safe. Do you know why I planned a picnic?"

"I am assuming the question is rhetorical?" She picked a piece of lint off the blanket. The blush faded from her cheeks.

Nick pointed at the clouds. "I heard it was possible to buy someone a star name. So I thought I would, and then we could see your star together. According to NASA, the buying of stars is more of a scam than real. And I didn't want to get you some meaningless paper certificate."

"You really wanted to buy me a star?"

He wanted to get her many things, but he couldn't buy her peace of mind or a world where people were always kind. He took her hand. "You have brought a little bit of heaven into my life, and a star was the only thing I could think of to share heaven with you. I thought you would be annoyed if I spent even fifty dollars on a fake certificate."

She scooted closer. "Even if it isn't real, thanks for wanting to buy me a star name. And I'm glad you didn't waste your money."

"I did find you something else. The ad on the website said, 'Keys celebrate the wisdom, joy, and optimism in life. They express independence, confidence, and power.' You have so much strength and have filled me with so much joy. When I saw the star key, I knew the pendant was meant for you." Nick pulled a necklace box from his pocket. His heart started to race. Never had he given a gift like this to anyone.

Zoe opened the box and let out a little gasp. "Oh, it is beautiful!"

She traced the diamonds in the star at the end of the key.

"May I?" Nick held out his hand. Zoe handed him the necklace, turned her back to him, and lifted her hair.

Nick worked the clasp on the chain, his hands shaking the slightest bit, betraying his nervousness. When the necklace was linked, he placed a kiss on the back of her neck and wrapped his arms around her waist. Zoe dropped her hair and leaned back into him. This woman brought a new meaning to heaven. He held her and listened to the rain, rehearsing one last time the words he'd planned to say. Zoe shifted.

Nick spoke before she could move out of his embrace. "In my grandmother's day, it was popular to get a promise ring or be pinned with your beau's frat pin as a sign the couple was going steady. My grandma told me a hundred times the story of Grandpa giving his pin to her. I'm not saying this very well. I think of this necklace as the key to my heart and a promise of more to come."

Zoe turned in his arms. Her fingers traced the pendant resting at the base of her neck. "Are you trying to ask me to be your girl?"

He couldn't resist kissing her before answering. "Something like that. It means taking our relationship public as soon as you are ready. The downside of money is the fame. New York provides a bit of anonymity as there is always someone more famous than you. Our first two or three times at events will draw the most speculation and press. You and I both need to know if this lifestyle is one you can live. So far you haven't experienced the public side." It wouldn't be easy. She would lose some privacy as, eventually, she would need her own driver and bodyguard. People would take her photo just because she was there.

Zoe placed her hand on his cheek. "Given my reservations about you being a billionaire, that is understandable. I think I can handle it. I've watched some of my friends figure out the nine-zeros-club lifestyle this year. Abbie is the funniest—drives her bodyguards crazy. I'll have to have them at some point, won't I?"

Nick nodded gratefully. She knew in part what he was asking.

She dropped her hand and retraced the key. "I saw this in the store the other day when I was with Mandy and Tessa. I do want to keep it, but there is no way I am going to wear diamonds on the subway."

"Good thing I got you this." Nick took a velvet bag from another pocket. "It is a smaller version in silver with no diamonds. Subway and work safe."

Zoe set the bag on her lap, then leaned in and kissed him. She pulled back and whispered, "In case you are wondering … Yes, I'll be your girl."

Nick pulled her back to him to finish what she'd started. He was going to enjoy her being his girl. Halfway through the kiss, his stomach made a mortifying rumble. Zoe began to giggle, and the kiss ended.

"I guess that means we have had enough dessert." Zoe opened the basket and started to pull out the food.

No, he hadn't had enough dessert. There would be more moments to share like this, and he looked forward to them all.

twenty

FRIDAY MORNING, ZOE WALKED TO the subway, wondering if it would be the last time. Once she was recognized, she would have to quit. Fortunately, commuters rarely looked at each other. Tonight, they would attend her favorite musical to end a perfect week. Her parents were thrilled she was dating, the job as a junior designer was hers, and Nick fit every dream of finding her Prince Charming. His morning texts started each day with a smile.

Last night they'd attended their first public event—a small opening of a new museum exhibit. Photographers yelled for his attention for a photo. With his arm around her waist, Nick posed. Zoe smiled but didn't talk to any reporters. She would wait for PR to release a statement, which could understandably make work interesting today.

The car was half empty. After checking to make sure no one needed the vacant seat, she took it and opened her phone to the news app, wondering if any of the photos the paparazzi shot last night had found their way into the news. She clamped her hand over her mouth to prevent a scream. If she had been standing, she may have fainted. They had to be wrong. She checked the *Times* and another national news outlet. The headlines all read the same.

"Nick Gooding Accused of Sexual Assault"

One of the news outlets ran the photo from last night's event. A mistake! A lie! Every time she tried to get past the headline, her vision blurred. She made it to the office and into her new pod cubicle.

April stopped in, her eyes flashing. "You do this to everyone?" She punctuated the question mark as if thrusting a sword.

"Do what?"

"Accuse them—" April signed a sign Zoe was unfamiliar with. She guessed it had to do with the assault. "Liar," April yelled the word as she signed.

April turned and left.

Zoe sat paralyzed. Something was very wrong. Bile rose in her throat. She ran to the bathroom and away from the eyes of her coworkers.

She rested her head against the cold metal door, half wishing she had her phone and half glad she didn't.

The door opened, and she heard three sets of footsteps.

A woman spoke. "I bet she gave him the shiner the press has been speculating about. I always knew Goodie-Two-Shoes Gooding was too good to be true. And the papers still making him out to be some saint."

"The press could be wrong. The photo of them together doesn't make sense. They look happy." The voice may have been Gina's.

"The article I read said it isn't the first time she's brought up false charges. Two years ago in Indiana—" There was no mistaking the oddly flat intonations of April's voice.

Zoe covered her ears.

When she removed her hands, the voices were gone.

She slipped out of the bathroom and to the elevator, avoiding her desk and phone. She had a twenty and her subway card. She could get someplace with that.

The conference room resembled a zoo with all the animals stuck in one cage. Two lawyers; the head of Gooding's security; Maurene from Scott & Ricks, along with her subordinates; a detective from the NYPD; and the head of a private-investigation agency alternately yelled into phones and at each other.

Several whiteboards flanked the room. Nick watched the work around him in a daze. The headline burned into his retina an hour ago was the subject of everyone's conversation. An invisible slime covered him. He wanted to go home and shower, hide in his man cave, and never come out. Perhaps eat a dozen of Mom's famous snicker-doodles. People believed he could be *that man*. Generations of Goodings in this city and not a single news outlet argued the possibility that he was innocent, that a mistake had been made, or even the possibility that another man shared his name.

Despite his innocence, a feeling of impending doom clouded the room. Had this been what Zoe felt when social media bullies had attached the woman-who-cried-wolf opinion page to her name? Only for her it never ended. This would end for him. He had the resources to find the truth.

He didn't believe the story claiming Zoe was his accuser any more than he thought he had been accused. His texts and calls had been met with silence. When Maurene arrived, she had told him Zoe's phone and bag had been found sitting on her desk, but no one had seen her. The building's security tape showed her leaving the building about a half hour after she arrived. She appeared to be alone.

Nick wished himself out of the room so he could join Sebastian and his team in their search for her. But he was stuck here waiting for a text or call that Zoe was safe. Zoe, where are you? He sent up a silent prayer for her safety.

The only bright piece of news so far was the detective from the NYPD who couldn't find a valid warrant for Nick's arrest. Two uniformed officers sat in the lobby, supposedly for his protection. He could feel them waiting to pounce and bring down one of the country's wealthiest men.

Phones rang. Hands flew over computer keys. The only thing the room lacked was a giant ticking clock. The digital display on his phone was bad enough. One hour turned into another.

"Bingo!" someone yelled from behind a computer. "A Nicholas D. Gooding of Wisconsin, age forty-five, has a warrant out for his arrest after a victim named him perpetrator during an interview in the ER of the local hospital." Clapping filled the room. Nick took his first deep breath since arriving at work.

He ran his hands down his face. The knot in his stomach loosened. The false accusations would be yesterday's news in a week or less.

One of the PR people called Maurene over. "A Wisconsin news station found the accuser, Zoe, or rather, *ZoElle* Watson. They are camping out on her front lawn. Unfortunately, they haven't realized their mistake about the Mr. Goodings yet." Maurene put the news feed up on one of the monitors.

"Poor woman. How did they even get her name? Isn't the victim's identity supposed to be kept private?" Nick looked at the NYPD detective for confirmation.

"It should be. Well, my work is done here. I hope you get the rest of this cleared up soon." The detective left, taking with him some more of the gloom.

Nick gathered his things, he could leave. His father approached.

"Son I know you want to run out and comb the streets for her, but you won't make it ten feet before you are bombarded. Let our guys do the searching."

Nick caught the flash of a woman's face as she slammed the door on a reporter. Maybe he couldn't find Zoe at the moment, but he could do something to help the other woman. He went into the office and dialed Daniel Crawford's private cell. He skipped all pleasantries. "I need the number for your security firm. I'll explain later."

Nick dialed the number Daniel gave him.

"Good afternoon, Hastings Security."

"Jethro Hastings, please. It's a matter of some urgency."

"Whom may I say is calling?"

"Nick Gooding. Daniel Crawford recommended your firm."

"Mr. Hastings is not on the premises. I am directing your call to Mr. Alan."

"Wait, no—" Nick's protest was too slow, and background music began playing in his ear.

"This is Mr. Alan."

"I'm sorry. Daniel told me to be sure to speak with one of the Hastings."

"I'm Alan Hastings. Does that help?"

"It depends. Is your sister Abbie?"

"You know Abbie?"

"Yes. Now, I need one of your best men to get up to Wisconsin as soon as he can."

Nothing she could find on the library computer helped. The media had dropped her name from the stories and replaced it with some poor woman's from Wisconsin or, in the case of the larger outlets, declined to use any name, mentioning only that Mr. Goodings accuser was not the woman shown in an earlier photo. But the damage was done. At least one pseudo-news blog site had connected her campus newspaper and Mr. Dodd's assault reports. Now some outlets questioned why Nick would associate with a person who would lie about an assault. Yesterday, the office rumor had been that Mr. Dodd had planned to appear in court today and plead guilty to several charges. The feed of a small New York city court–watching site claimed a plea deal was now unlikely.

A screen pop-up informed her that her half hour had ended and she needed to relinquish the computer for others to use. Zoe left the computer and went and signed up for another half-hour slot. She would have to wait an hour and a half.

She found a chair in the teen section and grabbed the nearest book. The dictionary would have been a better choice as not a word made it past her retinas and into her brain.

After a minute, she got up and asked a librarian for a paper and pen.

She sat at a table and wrote.

> Nick,
>
> My heart keeps telling me my eyes are lying. My brain is yelling at me to run. Now my life is bare for the world to see. People are questioning why you would associate with me. And why I would mar the Gooding name.
>
> You said the other night we needed to figure out if I could deal with the media.
>
> I am not as brave as you believe, I am not stronger than I seem, and I'm not smarter than you think.
>
> I'm sorry.
>
> Zoe
>
> PS. I know you are innocent of the charges.

Zoe went into a stall in the bathroom and pulled the diamond-key necklace out of the lining of her bra. She hadn't dared leave it lying around the apartment. She hesitated before removing the less-expensive silver necklace from around her neck. She should return them both. But she couldn't. He had given her the key to her own heart as well.

Zoe folded the note grade-school style until it became an envelope, then put the diamond necklace inside.

In the lobby of the Goodings' office building, Zoe stopped at the information desk.

"I have a delivery for Nick Gooding."

The receptionist paid her little attention. "You and every other woman in New York."

"Please see that he gets it. It has something he will want back."

At twenty minutes to five, the head of building security rushed into Nick Gooding's office with a $16,000 diamond-key necklace and handwritten note that had been dropped off at the lobby information desk four hours earlier.

"How was she not noticed?"

"According to the cameras, she had on a coat with the hood up. The receptionist working the desk had been dealing with an excessive amount of women looking for you delivering gifts, flowers, or paternity suits. Our employee claims not to even have gotten a good look at the person who delivered the note. She put it in the bin. We discovered the necklace during a routine X-ray of the contents of the hand deliveries."

"Anything else?"

"No. I'll return if you don't need anything. We still have quite a few envelopes and packages to scan." The guard left the room more slowly than he entered it.

Nick walked to the window and leaned on the pane. Below him, 8.5 million people hurried about their lives. How could he find one lost woman? There had been no other report of her from any of the security personnel or private investigators he had sent to find her. Zoe hadn't returned to her apartment or work. Sean and Tessa hadn't heard from her either. What-ifs flooded him. Without her phone, she didn't have a map app. Zoe could be anyplace and not have any idea she was in the wrong part of town.

An hour later, building security from Scott & Ricks called. "Mr. Gooding, Zoe Wilson just left the building after going to her desk. As you requested, no one stopped her. One of your men is now tailing her."

A text came in a moment later from one of the bodyguards. **Following Z on subway.**

Relief filled him. He called only to be routed to voicemail. He was tempted to call Sebastian and meet Zoe at the apartment, but the words of her note stared up at him from his desk. Perhaps it was best not to go rushing in yet. At least he knew she was safe.

That wasn't good enough.

Against Sebastian's advice, Nick rang the buzzer to Zoe's apartment again.

She didn't answer.

twenty-one

Last night, Zoe sent two brief messages, one to Candace, and one to her mother, before turning off her phone. Ignoring Nick's text to call him was a choice that brought her to tears. She didn't remember changing out of her work clothing or if she had eaten.

Judging by the sun streaming through her window, that had been more than twelve hours ago. It was useless to believe getting out of bed would make things better. She had no energy. Her mind ticked through the things her therapist had suggested. She dismissed each one. Perhaps if she stayed in bed long enough, the pain and humiliation would all go away. Some other terrible thing would happen in the world, and people would move on. Had Nick's name been cleared yet? She didn't dare turn on her phone or computer to find out. If she could hide out for thirty-six hours, the news would move on to a more profitable story.

The door buzzer rang again. It had rung several times last night. She pretended not to hear it.

Someone knocked on her door. Another tenant must have let her visitor in. Probably Mrs. Clark.

The door rattled, then Tessa's voice echoed through the apartment. "Zoe, you come undo the security lock right now or I will break down the door, and as your landlord, I'll charge you for the damage."

Zoe pushed back the covers, plodded to the door, and flipped back the lock.

Tessa came in and slammed the door. She held her phone to her ear. "She is here … No … I'll call you."

Zoe left Tessa there and went back to her bedroom, where she sat on the bed. She stared at the rag doll in her hands, wondering when she'd taken it off the dresser.

Tessa didn't knock on the bedroom door. "Zoe Wilson, I don't know who is worse—you or your cousin. Do you have any idea how much worry you have caused everyone? We have been calling, texting, and emailing. Sean even called Mrs. Clark downstairs, and she said she hadn't heard you all morning or seen you come in. Nick was ready to call missing persons, but you were seen yesterday afternoon dropping off a note at the information desk, so he couldn't claim you had been missing twenty-four hours yet. If you hadn't put the diamond necklace in the note, I doubt it would have ever been opened. He worried that you'd evaded one of his bodyguards and managed to leave undetected last night."

Nick had someone watching her? "I texted Candace and my mom."

"Well, you are not the only Wilson woman to go AWOL this weekend. So texting Candace won't do you any good."

Zoe sat up. "What is wrong with Candace?"

"You mean other than Colin proposing and her running back to Art House with her wig in a twist?"

Zoe shook herself. Candace hadn't said anything the other night when they'd talked. "He proposed? I can't believe it."

Tessa sat down on the bed. "Not any more than I can believe you sitting in your bed and hiding from the world. What is wrong with you?"

"Shall I start with before or after I ruined Nick Gooding's life? People are questioning his judgment because of me and my past."

"Lies about your past."

Zoe ignored Tessa's interruption. "Or the fact Mr. Dodd changed his plea to not guilty because they found the college newspapers. Or maybe I just can't make it here or anywhere." Zoe stood and grabbed an armful of clothes, adding it to the suitcase she'd pulled out last night. "Country mouse in New York. What a joke. Oh, and don't forget the gossip. It was hard enough facing work a week ago. I can't do it again. It will probably push off my graduation, but I can't stay." Zoe stopped talking before she started to cry. *I am not as brave as you believe, I am not stronger than I seem, and I'm not smarter than you think. I can't do this again.*

Tessa grabbed the next batch of clothes from Zoe's hands. "I wish I could slap some sense into you the way they do in the old movies. Nick is worried sick about you. Even though the other Nick Gooding was caught late last night in Indiana, half the media outlets are still showing your Nick's picture because nothing is slower to come out than the truth if it won't sell well. You need to find your big-girl pants and put them back on. The only way this is going to end happily is if you and Nick face this together." Tessa's anger broke through Zoe's mind.

"I knew it wasn't my Nick." Her appearing with him wouldn't calm the media storm. She was still tainted. "What can I do? It isn't like the truth helped last time."

Tessa bent over the half-packed suitcase and pulled out a pair of jeans. "Start with a shower. Then text everyone and tell them you are fine."

Zoe took the jeans and shut herself in the bathroom. If only taking a shower could solve everything. The water splashing against the sides of the ancient tub mixed with her tears.

Nick tried to explain to the Japanese entrepreneur about his case of mistaken identity. It didn't help. The man still wanted out of his contract. Nick ended the call with a promise to have the necessary papers drawn up Monday morning.

His father came into his office. "Another one gone?"

"Sorry, Dad." Nick couldn't remember the last time his father had come into the office on a Saturday.

"If it is any consolation, the chairmen of two of the boards you are on have removed their threat to have you voted off."

Nick rubbed his temples. "Just when I thought the silver lining was getting out of some meetings."

Ansley sat down opposite his son. "Have you heard from Zoe yet?"

He shook his head. "Just Tessa. She went over to the apartment, but no details."

"What are you going to do?"

"What can I do? We got to the can-you-handle-the-media part of our relationship, and this happens. The most colossal media blunder of all time puts us both in the crosshairs." Nick checked his watch before taking another over-the-counter pain reliever. "It is going to take a week to even dig halfway out. If she doesn't want to meet me partway, I don't know that I can do anything."

"Reverend Cavanagh would tell you to pray."

"I know, Dad. It's just … I don't even know what to pray for." Was it selfish to pray that Zoe would come rushing back into his arms? Or would normal things like the serenity prayer be more appropriate? Praying for something more significant to hit the news and bury the story about him on a one-inch paragraph on page 37 crossed his mind, but few things outside of wars and natural disasters could bump the articles from the headlines, and he couldn't pray for those. In the end, he prayed for wisdom. After all, he felt that prayer had been answered last week as he sat on Zoe's couch holding a bag of berries to his eye.

"You'll figure it out. Why don't we close up for now?"

Nick glared at his silent phone one last time before putting it in his pocket and following his father to the elevator.

The shower helped. Zoe fluffed her hair and went to thank Tessa for her tough love.

She found Tessa in the kitchen cooking a pan of eggs. "Here, eat."

Zoe held out a plate while Tessa scooped the food onto it. "Thanks." The eggs smelled good and tasted even better. Either Zoe was hungrier than she realized, or Tessa's cooking skills had improved.

"While you are eating, you can fill me in on a few things. Like why you trusted a person at a general information desk to deliver a necklace worth twice as much as my old car to Nick. And then you can tell me why you had it in the first place."

"Because I said it was for him? And he gave it to me." Zoe stuffed a forkful of eggs into her mouth so she wouldn't have to answer for a while. She hadn't even told her mother or Candace the significance of the necklace, just that she was officially dating.

Tessa crossed her arms. "I am going to give you a pass on not thinking when you returned it. Yesterday was traumatic. Although you should have tried to see him. According to Sean, Nick has been worried about you all morning since you disappeared from work without even your phone. He would have gone searching for you himself if he hadn't had a couple of New York's finest watching him until they finally confirmed the mixed-up identities, by which time he couldn't sneeze without the nightly news reporting it. He deployed every off-duty security guard and bodyguard at his disposal to look for you. You at least owe him a phone call."

"You saw the news yesterday—what they said about him and me. What happens when someone realizes the 911 call was him? He is a Gooding. I feel like me knowing him has put mud all over

his name. If I step back now, maybe the damage won't be so bad."
She couldn't call or see him. Her resolve was not that strong.

"The damage to him or his reputation?" Tessa swirled a water bottle.

"Both."

The silence grew as Zoe choked down the last of her eggs.

"Over the past two years, I have learned some interesting things from being a member of the Art House. When it comes to men, we are all idiots. I nearly walked away from Sean because of my fear of long-distance relationships. Mandy didn't trust Daniel to be the person she knew him to be. Araceli didn't think she measured up and didn't stand up for herself. Abbie, well, she couldn't admit the truth. Then there is you and Candace. I want to shake you both."

"I want to shake Candace too." Zoe washed her plate off.

"You are as bad as she is!"

"No, I'm not. Colin proposed."

"And Nick didn't?"

"No."

Tessa's chair scraped back from the table. She stood at the end of the galley kitchen blocking Zoe in. "So giving you expensive jewelry and asking if you would be his girlfriend publicly was what?"

Zoe crossed her arms. "I believe it is called going steady."

"Aka an assumed engagement. He came here three times last night and again this morning. Stop being stupid and go after him."

"I can't."

"Why not?"

"Because if you love someone, you should let them go."

Tessa stood and left without a word. Zoe stared at the door. Tessa didn't come back. Zoe tried calling Candace and got voicemail. She studied Nick's contact information page for a while before pushing the green Call button. If he didn't answer, she would know he understood her note and agreed. The phone went to voicemail on the fourth ring. She left a message anyway.

The half-full suitcase waited in her room. She owed Scott & Ricks a formal resignation. She hung the clothes back in the closet. It would be cheaper to buy a ticket to Indianapolis with a two-week advance. She set the phone next to the rag doll and pretended she didn't care that Nick hadn't answered.

Nick listened to the voicemail that had been left while he was in the shower, again. *"Hi, Nick, I know I didn't handle yesterday very well. I am not sure what to say. Goodbye."* Zoe hadn't called since. He wasn't sure if he should return the call. At least she was safe. And was the goodbye a farewell for good or just how she ended a call? Tessa had been of little help ranting about stupid Wilson women before locking herself in her home studio with a computer. Sean had only shrugged his shoulders.

Most of the major news outlets had apologized for the story and recanted. A temporary secretary at the city police office wanting to earn a buck had been blamed. After seeing Nick's photo with Zoe on a social media post, she'd sold a partially redacted copy of the police report to a sleazy blog. No one could explain how the story got picked up nationally without due diligence. Alan Hastings called to let him know ZoElle, who preferred to be called Elle, had been relocated to a safe house since some people blamed her for the story and for ruining the Gooding name. Nick instructed Alan to cover whatever expenses he felt necessary, including engaging a lawyer and counselor. Elle wouldn't look back two years later and wonder why justice hadn't been served.

Zoe's tale, unfortunately, remained a story of interest, and the pundits argued over the "he said/she said" of the original story. Some analysts declared the school had handled the situation poorly, calling the man's side a case of "He doth protest too much." Stories of false accusations at other universities found their way back out of obscurity as Hollywood A-listers shot hashtags across cyberspace like well-aimed darts.

The latest report from the bodyguard watching the apartment was that Zoe hadn't ventured out all weekend. Although she had ordered a small batch of groceries. Better than a cab to JFK.

Late Sunday afternoon, Colin texted.

—Sorry I couldn't bury Zoe's life deeper.

Not your fault.

—Is she talking to you?

Nick debated about how real to make his answer. **She left me a goodbye note.**

—I'm not sure if the carousel will be finished anytime soon. The artist may or may not have quit.

Candace? Why?

—I proposed. I thought she was willing after she came back from Blue Pines. I guess I don't understand women.

You and me both, my friend.

— I was serious when I said it is easier to hack the Pentagon than it is to understand a woman.

My guess is that it's easier to hack North Korea's military servers.

Nick tried to think of the most outlandish thing he could.

— Nah. Only took me two hours.

Nick didn't dare ask any more questions. His phone pinged again.

— Just kidding. Haven't tried that one.

I'm relieved to know that. Don't.

— Not that desperate. I still have Mandy, the secret weapon. She's calling. Bye.

Nick checked the clock in his office. The Monday Tokyo stock market would open soon. It would be the first indicator of whether people believed in his innocence deep enough to feel it in their pocketbooks. He opted to watch rather than wake up to an unpleasant surprise. Besides, trying to sleep became an exercise in not thinking about Zoe. After three hours of watching Gooding Enterprises remain steady, Nick fell asleep on the couch and dreamed about Zoe.

twenty-two

GINA HAD REFUSED THE EMAIL resignation Zoe sent from the public library Friday afternoon, sending a reply that she expected Zoe in her office by eight thirty Monday morning. Waiting for the subway, Zoe was glad Gina hadn't accepted the resignation. Sometime Sunday afternoon, she'd started to feel like her old self again. Nick still hadn't returned her message. That didn't matter. No one was going to continue to steal her life from her. For too long she'd allowed that stupid TA to control what people thought of her. Some second-rate secretary in Wisconsin wasn't going to do the same. It may have helped that she'd received posts from three of her favorite movie stars supporting her.

She scrolled back through Nick's old messages until she found the one she wanted.

I'm a text away if you need me today. You are braver than you believe, stronger than you seem, and smarter than you think.

She changed the font size until it filled the window, then took a screenshot. Movement at the end of the platform caught her attention. She nodded at the bodyguard, and he nodded back. Nick might not be answering her message, but he cared enough to have her followed.

Passengers crowded into the car, all paying more attention to their phones than to her. Thankfully, the secretary of state had said something controversial, and his comments now topped the news, along with the hurricane brewing in the tropics. The bodyguard stood near the door. Zoe changed her home screen to Nick's text. She thought about texting him; however, *"Thanks for sending the bald guy to look out for me"* didn't explain it well, and "Thanks for still caring" was just lame. Zoe exited at her stop and didn't look back to see if her shadow had followed her.

The office space was finished. The painters and plasterers must have worked double time. The smells of new carpet and paint filled the air. A cup of steaming cider sat at her desk. Zoe looked for James but didn't see him. She read the sticky note on top of her whiteboard.

My office, ASAP. Gina (bring your cider)

Gina waved her in through the glass. "Close the door and sit down."

Zoe tried to relax.

"Next time you need a personal day, ask." Gina held up a finger and added a second. "I am assuming your resignation was from the stress of the moment, so it stays between us and has already been deleted from my system." A third finger joined the others. "I believe you told the truth about two years ago and about Mr. Dodd. That being said, I know not everyone does." Gina slid a business card across the desk. "This is my therapist. Go see her. She is covered 100 percent, and, in my opinion, is the best in the city."

Zoe took the card. "Thanks. I need a couple visits. Friday was brutal."

"I understand. Now, are you ready to get to work?"

Zoe nodded.

"Don't tell Adrian this, but if you only give your job 70 percent this week, I'll count your work as 110 percent." Gina stood.

"I need to go check on something in the break room, so if you want to use my phone to make a private call, you are welcome to."

The not-so-subtle push and the necessary privacy convinced Zoe to make an appointment for that evening. The therapist tried to work around her clients' hours. She had thought of setting up a video call with her old therapist, but a recommendation from Gina would be better.

Thanks to James being the lead designer of her pod, Zoe made it through the morning. He kept her supplied with meaningful work and another caramel cider.

After lunch, she received a meeting request from Maurene in PR. Zoe bit her lip and accepted the invitation.

A half hour later, she was ushered into a large office. A bank of muted TVs tuned to different stations covered one wall.

"Have a seat, Zoe. Don't worry. I won't bite. But I don't promise this won't be painless."

The couch was more comfortable than the uber-modern design looked. Maurene sat next to her in an armchair. "As you know, Scott & Ricks handles the Goodings' PR. I am sure you are aware of the current public-relations problem that exploded Friday and over the weekend."

Zoe started to open her mouth, but Maurene shook her head and continued. "There are three innocent victims we want to focus on. Nick Gooding, of course, Miss ZoElle Watson, and you. In fifteen minutes, Miss Watson has agreed to do a conference video call with you. From what I gather, you have been in a similar place to where she is right now. Both of you have a credibility problem that is largely the media's fault. We want to use them to correct their error but in a controlled way. Particularly, the women of America need to meet you and hear your story. I have booked you and Elle on a Wednesday morning show filmed here in New York. I trust the host and hostess. They will be giving you prescreened questions. Anything you don't like, you change. Elle has yet to agree. I think that is going to depend on if you can

155

manage to click with her during your call. The worst thing we can do is put you on stage together and have tension between you."

Maurene never asked Zoe if she agreed to sit in front of an audience of millions and bare her soul. Instead, the PR director continued as if Zoe's participation was a given. Zoe listened as Maurene outlined her plan, from what colors Zoe should wear to the interview, to instructions to wear her hair down to give her a softer look. Zoe thought about declining, but if this could help Elle and Nick, she would risk humiliation because Maurene believed it would work.

Finally, the video call started. Elle looked like Zoe felt. Haunted. They introduced themselves, and Zoe found she didn't know what to say next. Maurene slipped a paper in front of her. *Tell her about your weekend.*

"I'd say it doesn't get more awkward than this conversation, but we both lived through this weekend, so that would be a lie, wouldn't it? It was one of the most difficult of my life. One of my friends spent most of Saturday talking me out of making stupid choices."

Elle nodded. "The only good thing about this weekend is my bodyguard. I think I would not be here if not for him. I wanted to die so badly."

"I wanted to stay in bed and never leave."

"How did you handle it?"

"I watched a couple of inspirational videos from women who had a worse time than me. Went through some old exercises from my counselor, cried, prayed. That type of thing. In some ways, it is easier than two years ago. I had forgotten I needed to choose, not just be acted upon."

They fell into easy conversation. Near the end, Maurene told Elle about the interview. The pros and cons.

Elle bit her lip. "Can I meet Nick Gooding? I want to apologize."

"No apology necessary. He knows it wasn't your fault, but I am sure I can arrange a meeting," said Maurene.

"Then I'll come."

"Good, I'll see you tomorrow afternoon. We'll do some show prep."

The video link ended.

Maurene typed on her computer. I have scheduled you from three to six tomorrow and Wednesday until noon. Bring me a photo of a couple different outfits you have. Remember, it will be Halloween Wednesday, so absolutely no orange or black.

Zoe returned to her desk, not entirely able to concentrate on her day. Fear and determination fought for dominance. She unlocked her drawer and turned on the phone, reading Nick's text again. Determination won another round.

When Sebastian stopped in front of the Rockefeller center, Nick climbed out and headed for the familiar studio. He still wasn't sure why he had let himself be talked into a TV interview. Maurene assured him it would do wonders to rebuild the damage the false accusations had caused his reputation as well as that of Elle and Zoe. Of course, Maurene had him at Zoe. A witch on a scooter sped by, nearly mowing him down. Halloween morning in the city.

He checked in and proceeded directly to the green room. The show in progress was streamed to the large monitor on the wall. Someone dabbed powder on his face and concealer on the light bruising around his eye. Someone else connected the mic. Nick closed his eyes and took a moment to find a quiet place in his thoughts. He became aware of the interview playing on the television monitor. Why hadn't Maurene told him they were being interviewed? Elle answered a question, and the camera panned out.

The host asked his next question. "Zoe, how did you feel when you first saw your name in the news Friday morning?"

"Instantly, I was back in the campus library study room, a hand covering my mouth to stifle my screams, helpless to prevent what was happening to me. Only this time, I didn't have my innocence to lose. I only had love. The media's lies are just as violating as what I experienced on campus. The hardest part is this time I can't stand and face my nameless, faceless perpetrators and ask them to pay for their crimes. Or demand they repair the damage they did to me, to Elle, and to Nick Gooding. The news cycle will move on to the next story while we attempt to rebuild our lives and our reputations. And the story will never really go away, will it?"

There was a space of silence when she finished talking. *I only had love.* Did she mean him? He shouldn't have listened to the advice he had been given. He should have camped out on the front stoop if that was what it took. Nick ran across the room to the sound-stage door. A burly bodyguard blocked his path.

"I need to get in there."

"Sorry, Mr. Gooding. I have my orders. No one enters while the red light is on."

"But—"

The guard didn't budge.

On TV, the host segued into a commercial break. The producer stepped through the door. "Mr. Gooding, if you will come with me."

The couch where Zoe and Elle had sat was empty. The producer sat him in the corner nearest the host. There was a quick light check, a thumbs up, and the theme music played.

"Thank you for joining us this morning to talk about the biggest media blunder since Truman won the presidency over Dewey." The famous photo of President Truman holding a newspaper declaring Dewey the winner filled the screen behind the host and the questions began.

"If you had one takeaway from this debacle, what would it be?" asked the hostess.

"Don't spread gossip. Multiple people—from professionals employed by various national and international news agencies to bloggers and social media posters—failed to check even the simplest of facts. The impossibility of me being in Wisconsin wasn't brought out until my team of lawyers started making phone calls and tossing words like *defamation* and *libel* around. Several so-called news organizations—not this network, I understand—published the name of the victim, which has long been against policy. Not only that, they published the wrong name. In the name of free speech, two women were assaulted each time someone reposted an inaccurate news story or created a meme. Talk-show hosts and social-media juries ripped the humanity from not only Elle's and Zoe's lives but from their own as well. Today humanity is a little less humane than we were a week ago. Gossip at the speed of light is more harmful than gossip at the speed of a whisper ever was."

The host wrapped up the show, and the credit music played. Aware the cameras were still on him, Nick remained where he was. He did remove his mic and make sure it was off before asking. "Where is Zoe?"

"I believe she left."

Nick took off his mic and handed it to the nearest technician. He had to find her.

Zoe and Elle held each other and cried as Nick's defense of them played on the screen in the little viewing room they had been ushered into after they left the stage. He kept turning the questions around so they weren't about him or his struggle. Zoe wished her answer had been half as eloquent. At least she had stopped short of pointing out that the debacle had cost her a relationship with Nick. The subway bodyguard had followed her every night and morning. She almost felt terrible slipping into the back alley and taking a taxi to meet her new therapist. She wanted to talk to Nick in person about things, not have them reported by a third party.

Zoe handed Elle the box of tissue and took one for herself. She dabbed at her makeup, not wanting to smudge it too badly. In a few minutes, she would see Nick face-to-face as Maurene was bound to bring him in here also.

Elle held out her mascara-covered tissue. "Best makeup job I've had in my life and I am crying it all away. At least my body-guard isn't in here. I'm afraid he already thinks I am going to fly apart at any moment. I'm really not. I just need some quiet time to process."

Zoe looked at the door, where the guard stood on the other side. "What did you say his name was? He looks familiar."

"Mr. Alan. His real last name is Hastings. He has a lot of broth-ers or something."

"Adam, Alex, and Andrew. Only three."

"You know him?" Elle's interest was piqued.

Zoe thought she shouldn't encourage Elle's obvious crush. "Not well. He is usually behind the computer. I know his sister."

"Oh. She married a Preston Harmon, didn't she? Did you meet them because of Nick?"

Voices echoed in the hall, saving Zoe from explaining how she knew Abbie. The door opened, and Maurene entered. Nick was not with her. Zoe's heart sank a little. "Well done, ladies. Before I forget, Gina texted. Take the rest of the day as a comp day."

As soon as she got her phone and purse back from the check-room, she would text Gina a big thank-you.

"Elle, I have arranged for you to meet with Mr. Gooding at his office before lunch. We do have a choice to make. One of the afternoon's talk shows opened a fifteen-minute slot if you would like to take it. Apparently they feel your message is more impor-tant than dental hygiene on Halloween."

Perhaps she wouldn't text Gina a thank-you after all. "Do you have any other surprises planned for the afternoon show?"

"Surprises?"

"Yes, like enter Nick Gooding stage left while we are whisked away stage right."

"No, we had to do it that way. He didn't know you would be on either." Maurene nodded as if to finalize the confirmation, then walked out of the room. The women followed under the protective eye of Mr. Alan.

Zoe peered down all the halls, hoping to see Nick and dreading she would have nothing to say if she did.

twenty-three

ZOE WANDERED AROUND MACY'S WHILE she waited for Elle to have her meeting with Nick. As she wove around the jewelry counter, a pair of cuff links caught her eye. She pulled out her credit card and bought them before she lost her nerve.

Then she found a semiprivate corner and dialed Sebastian's number.

"Hi, this is Zoe. It isn't an emergency, but I need your help." Zoe outlined her plan. Sebastian approved.

When Maurene appeared with Elle, Zoe ended the call.

"Let's get you both new blouses before the show."

Elle looked around her. "I can't—"

Maurene waved her off. "No, this is on our bill. PR stuff."

They spent the next half hour finding clothes before they were driven back to Rockefeller Center and another studio. This time they took selfies after finishing with hair and makeup. Elle was right about the best makeup job of her life. Zoe wished she knew how the artist had put on her concealer.

The comedian-turned-hostess kept most of her questions on the lighter side—impressing on the audience the need to quickly report crimes and commending Elle and Zoe for their bravery. The subject of the media turning lives upside down never came up. Nor did anything of depth. Zoe wondered if the interview was a waste of time. In the end, the hostess lobbed a question about the importance of self-defense to Zoe to transition into her next guest—a self-defense expert. Even that question only required a one-word answer.

When they finished, Maurene met them in the green room. "Good show, ladies. I'll have the driver take Elle and her bodyguard to the airport. Zoe, do you need a ride?"

"No, thank you." Zoe gave Elle one last hug. "Call me if you need to talk." She shook hands with Alan. "If Elle loses my number, your sister has it. You have my permission to get my number from her."

Alan nodded once, then straightened. Zoe recognized the look from Abbie. He had shifted to full bodyguard mode. Zoe went in search of Sebastian.

He was standing by his car. "Nice to see you, Zoe."

Zoe gave him a hug. "Not as nice as it is to see you. Please tell me this will work."

"I'm a driver, not a fortune-teller. However, I have been known to place a bet now and then. And I'd say the odds are in your favor."

Zoe slid into the car and prayed Sebastian was correct.

Nick turned off the TV. The afternoon's program had been more fluff than news. It would be good for Elle and Zoe to have this exposure. Housewives across America would rally for them and stop sharing the false stories. The intercom buzzed. He pushed the button.

"Your lawyer is on line two."

"Thanks."

Nick sat down before picking up the call. Only then did he realize he didn't know which lawyer. To the best of his knowledge, there wasn't a reason for any of his lawyers to be calling. "Nick Gooding."

"It's David. The assistant district attorney gave me a courtesy call. Wayne Dodd took a plea deal when another victim came forward after seeing the morning news show. He will be incarcerated for a minimum of fifteen years."

"I thought his lawyers were busy looking for loopholes and ways to turn Zoe's story into coleslaw."

"The last victim to come forward has very compelling DNA evidence—in the form of a six-year-old son. The assault happened before Dodd took a job with Scott & Ricks. And after today's talk-show rounds, they doubted they could get a sympathetic jury after all."

"Thanks for letting me know." Nick wondered how this latest victim had survived the last seven years. There were so many stories. So many broken hearts and lives.

Zoe would be happy to know she didn't need to endure another trial. He wondered how he should tell her. This news was for a face-to-face, someplace where there would not be trick-or-treaters. He hit the intercom button. "I'm wrapping things up here. Will you call Sebastian?"

Nick was halfway to the elevator when his assistant stopped him. "Sebastian says he will be here in fifteen to twenty. Something about Halloween."

He stopped at the atrium on his way down. Today he could see half of New Jersey. He needed to bring Zoe back here to watch a sunset.

Sebastian pulled over. "Just keep walking around the block. You can switch directions if you get dizzy. Just don't cross a street or go into any stores. I don't want you really lost." Zoe hopped out of the car.

Zoe circled the block, mingling with the employees rushing home early to get their little goblins and ghouls to the neighborhood party or find a party of their own.

Three honks—two short and one long. At the signal, Zoe searched the traffic for Sebastian's car.

Nick climbed out, yelling her name. "Are you lost?"

Not anymore.

She tried not to look at Sebastian as she slid into the center of the back seat.

"How did you end up over here?" Nick shut his door and nodded to Sebastian.

"I think the driver let me off at the wrong corner."

"You realize you are almost two miles from your place?"

"That's not far."

"It is on Halloween night. There is a reason every first responder in the city is tense tonight. Not the night to go walking half of Manhattan."

"Thanks for rescuing me."

At her cue, Sebastian closed the center window.

Nick looked from her to the window and back again, his eyebrows raised in question.

"Just so you know, the driver who left me there is in the front seat of this car. I've been walking around the block, waiting for you. I needed to talk, and I didn't know how or where." Zoe pulled a wrapped box out of her bag and handed it to Nick.

As he unwrapped the box, the tension around his eyes eased. He lifted the lid and revealed a pair of cuff links with tiny compasses engraved on the front.

"This is as close to finding a way to pin you as I could get. I chose the compasses because I have never felt lost as long as I knew you were around. Even the weekend I gave you the black eye, I wasn't lost. But when I let you go on Friday, I didn't know how to find my way back."

Nick held out his wrist. Zoe changed out the cuff links.

"Does this mean you'll wear the necklace again?"

Zoe nodded.

Nick made a spinning motion with his finger. Her skin came

alive as he gently placed the necklace around her neck once again. The pendant was warm against her skin. Where ever he had been keeping the jewelry, it must have been close to his heart. His fingers brushed over the back of her neck, sending a delightful tingle down her spine. Zoe dropped her hair. Nick didn't move back. His fingers trailed along her shoulders and down her arms. He leaned closer and whispered in her ear. "You have no idea how much I want to kiss you right now."

Zoe turned her head enough to see his profile. "Why don't you?"

Nick's gaze flicked to the front of the car and back.

"Audience? I thought this type of car had a privacy window."

"He'll still know we are kissing." His breath tickled her ear.

"So?" Zoe waited for him to respond, hoping he wouldn't care.

"When I was sixteen, Sebastian caught me kissing a girl in the back seat and gave me a lecture that scared the girl out of ever talking to me again."

Zoe tilted her head to try to see Nick's expression in the fading evening light. "What did he say?"

"He said the next girl he caught me kissing in his back seat better be the one I planned on taking to the altar."

She didn't dare move. Was he saying what she thought he was? *Oh please, please, please.*

For a moment, Zoe didn't move. Nick held his breath.

Then she turned to face him as much as she could in the confines of the seat belt. "Was that a proposal?"

Nick brought his hand up to cup her face. "It depends."

"On what?"

"On if you kiss me back."

Zoe laid her hand on his chest and leaned in. A mechanical hum stopped her. Sebastian winked in the review mirror as the black barrier continued to roll up.

"Does that mean I meet Sebastian's approval?" Zoe turned back to him.

"No, it means I did." Nick brushed his lips across hers. "You are over sixteen, right?"

Zoe pulled back an inch and cocked her head. Nick slid his hand down the seat, looking for her seat-belt release as well as his. "In this state, you don't have to wear a seat belt after the age of sixteen." Zoe slid the restraint off her shoulder and closed the gap between them. Nick looked into one eye, then the other, before lowering his gaze to Zoe's lips, which curled up in a smile. He lowered his head, and she met him halfway. Sebastian took a turn too fast, forcing Nick to hold Zoe closer.

Zoe giggled and whispered something against his lips about giving his driver a raise. Nick answered her with another kiss and hoped they were taking the long way home.

Epilogue

ZOE SAT NEXT TO NICK in the crowded theater. Every resident of Blue Pines who had been an extra or a gofer for the Hearthfire film had claimed a seat for the opening. Sean's grandfather had come up from Florida for the occasion and now sat with the newlyweds in the center of their row. Candace held hands with Colin in seats on the far side of Mandy and Daniel. Zoe couldn't wait to show her the ring hiding under her glove.

The director from Hearthfire stood in front of the stage droning on about how beautiful the town of Blue Pines had been for the filming and thanking the museum foundation and the Cavanaghs for supporting Hearthfire with this opening. Zoe rolled her eyes as Tessa winked back. The director didn't have a clue. Mandy's distinct laugh floated down the row as the lights dimmed.

Nick tugged at her gloves. She helped him get them off, enjoying the shivers he sent up her arms when he held her hand. More than once, she was distracted as he traced stars and hearts on the inside of her wrist.

Halfway through the movie, over the right shoulder of the male lead, Sean and Tessa shared their first kiss. Catcalls and whistles filled the theater.

Zoe wished she could see the director's face.

A slow pan of the square stopped on the Nativity church.

Nick rested his chin on her shoulder. "I'd like to get married there."

"Will you fly my family out?"

"Of course."

Zoe turned and kissed Nick briefly. The person behind them cleared their throat.

On the screen, the lead actor and actress kissed against a background of lightly falling snow.

Nick pulled the hair away from her ear and whispered. "Christmas? Reverend Cavanagh?"

"Sounds perfect."

The person behind them shushed them as the credits started to roll.

Zoe turned and kissed Nick on the cheek just to bug whoever it was.

When the lights came up, the octogenarian woman behind them bopped Nick over the head with her gloves. "Nick Gooding, is that you? Kissing in the theater? You should be ashamed of yourself."

Nick brought Zoe's left hand to his mouth and kissed her ring finger.

"Hey! Nick Gooding is engaged!" the woman shouted with all the volume of a baseball umpire.

Zoe felt her cheeks start to burn. This wasn't how they'd planned to tell their friends or the world.

To the cheers all around them, Nick lowered his head and kissed her. He had been right. Art House didn't have a curse, it had a blessing. Zoe kissed Nick back. This was infinitely better than a Hearthfire ending.

The End

acknowledgments

FOR ALMOST THIRTY YEARS OF my life I have been a graphic designer. It was fun to put Zoe in a dream job I never got. As always my books need a lot of help to get from my head and into your hands.

Tammy and Nanette are so willing to help make all my projects better and to read things so many times even in late night texts. I would never make it through a day without Sally and Cindy whose advice keeps me going. Thank you wonderful ladies.

Thanks also to Valerie B for her edits and Michele at Eschler Editing for her edits and finding oh so many little things to fix; any mistakes left in this book are not her fault. Nor are my excellent proofreaders to be blamed. Thank you ladies and gents!

My family, for sharing their home with the fictional characters who often got fed better than they did. And my husband who encourages me every crazy step of the way and puts up with all my messy spreadsheets.

And to my Father in Heaven for putting these wonderful people, and any I may have forgotten to mention, in my life. I am grateful for every experience and blessing I have been granted.

about the author

LORIN GRACE WAS BORN IN Colorado and has been moving around the country ever since, living in eight states and several imaginary worlds. She graduated from Brigham Young University with a degree in Graphic Design.

Currently she lives in northern Utah with her husband, four children, and a dog who is insanely jealous of her laptop. When not writing, Lorin enjoys creating graphics, visiting historical sites, museums, and reading.

LORIN IS AN ACTIVE MEMBER of the League of Utah Writers and was awarded Honorable Mention in their 2016 creative writing contest short romance story category. Her debut novel, *Waking Lucy,* was awarded a 2017 Recommended Read award in the LUW Published book contest. In 2018 the first book in this series, Mending Fences with the Billionaire, also received a Recommended Read award.

You can learn more about her, and sign up for her writers club at loringrace.com or at Facebook: LorinGraceWriter

www.ingramcontent.com/pod-product-compliance
Lightning Source LLC
Chambersburg PA
CBHW070525260626
47161CB00004B/1634